GARDNER

The Case of the
Waylaid Wolf

Erle Stanley Gardner

BALLANTINE BOOKS • NEW YORK

Foreword

For some years now I have been dedicating my Perry Mason books to outstanding figures in the field of legal medicine. Exceptional circumstances cause me to depart from this custom so that I can dedicate this book to a man who has done much to improve the administration of justice in this country.

Park Street, an attorney of San Antonio, Texas, is a member of the board of investigators and one of counsel of the Court of Last Resort.

On the occasion of writing this foreword Park Street is opening a "Perry Mason Room" in his suite of law offices. This room is dedicated not so much to Perry Mason but to the ideals Perry Mason stands for: unswerving loyalty to his clients, a devotion to the cause of justice, and an indomitable fighting spirit.

These are qualities that any good attorney has.

There are, of course, some attorneys whose definition of justice is measured in any given case by terms of expediency on the one hand and financial remuneration on the other.

These attorneys fortunately are in the minority. The overwhelming majority of lawyers in this country realize that they are officers of the court; that they are the high priests and priestesses in the temple of justice; that their duty is to their clients, to the courts and to the public. Having once embarked upon a case, they will fight to the last ditch with unswerving loyalty to their clients and to their ideals.

Perry Mason is, of course, a fictitious character. There are times when his loyalty to his clients and to the cause of justice leads him to take desperate chances. Attorneys who occasionally question his ethics still admire his loyalty and his sheer fighting ability. It is for these reasons that Park Street has dedicated a room to Perry Mason.

For some ten years now, in the Court of Last Resort, I have had the privilege of associating with a group of individuals who are devoting much of their time and energy trying to get the public to take a more active and understanding interest in the administration of justice. The bonds of friendship forged in the fires of fighting for a worthwhile objective are close indeed. During the years that I have been associated with Park Street, I have come to know him intimately. We have had many adventures together in the field of law and in investigating cases where innocent persons have been wrongfully convicted of crime.

And so, as the person who chronicles the adventures of Perry Mason, it gives me great pleasure to accede to Perry Mason's request to write this foreword as the first official document to be typed in Park Street's new Perry Mason Room, and to dedicate this book to a lawyer who has unswerving loyalty to his clients, who has for years cheerfully given both his time and money to advance the cause of justice, who is a loyal friend, an able attorney and a public-spirited citizen.

To my friend, PARK STREET.

—ERLE STANLEY GARDNER

Cast of Characters

I'tsen ved vallom e'nbcq ekovab. Seno... wasn'i
135 to veol gni noa saffron.
IV-156. E.1. pitang 1415 thi.polloffand gavanged
139

Chapter 1

It had started to rain that morning when Arlene Ferris parked her car in the fenced-off parking lot reserved for employees in the executive offices of the Lamont Rolling, Casting and Engineering Company.

The precipitation was a cold, wintry rain, and Arlene rolled up the windows of her car, bundled her raincoat about her and walked briskly to the side entrance marked *Employees Only*.

It was still raining at noon, but there was no necessity for Arlene to leave the building since the employees of the executive offices were able to use the underground tunnel to the cafeteria in the main building.

At quitting time Arlene was in the midst of work on some specifications which she knew should go out in the night's mail. It would take her about thirty minutes to finish up, but since Arlene was never one to watch the clock on a secretarial job, she pounded away at the typewriter, heedless of the exodus of other employees.

When she handed in the work to George Albert, the office manager, he glanced at the clock and was gratefully surprised.

"Thank you very much, Miss Ferris," he said.

"Not at all. I realized these should be in the mail tonight."

"Not all of our girls are that considerate. We certainly appreciate your loyalty to the job. It surprised me you were willing to waive overtime."

"A good job is worth being loyal to," she said, and wished him good night.

The rain had turned into a cold drizzle. Reflected lights shimmered on the wet paving of the parking lot. Arlene hurried to her car, opened the door, got in, turned the key and stepped on the starter.

Sometimes the car took a little longer to start on cold, rainy nights, so she wasn't too concerned at first when the only sound which emanated from underneath the hood was the grind of the battery-driven starter with no explosive response from the motor.

After the first minute and a half, she became distinctly worried and looked around at the now all but deserted parking place. Only a few cars were spotted here and there, and Arlene suddenly realized that her battery was not turning the motor as fast as it had been. Her car seemed definitely stalled.

Suddenly a cheerfully competent voice said, "What's the matter? Having trouble?"

Arlene rolled down the left window to inspect the smiling, confident eyes of the tall, broad-shouldered man whose raincoat was belted about his trim waist.

"I seem to be having trouble with my motor," she said.

"Better let the battery rest for a minute," the man said. "You're not doing any good, just grinding away at it. Let me take a look."

He stepped to the side of the motor, raised the hood professionally, plunged his head and shoulders inside, then emerged after a moment and said, "Watch my right hand. When I wave it, press the starter. When I move it down sharply, stop. Be sure the ignition key is turned to the 'on' position. All ready?"

Arlene nodded gratefully.

Once more the head and shoulders vanished from sight. She watched the right hand. It waved gently, and Arlene pressed the starter. Almost at once the hand was plunged downward in a swiftly emphatic gesture, and Arlene took her foot off the starter.

The man lowered the hood of the car, walked around and shook his head. "No spark," he said.

"What does that mean?"

"Something's definitely wrong with your electrical system. There's no use running down your battery by using the starter. You're just not getting any current to the spark plugs.

2

I'm afraid there's not much I can do in the rain. With the hood up, water keeps dripping down on the distributing system—that's probably what's the matter with it anyhow. I think you'd better leave it right here tonight. By tomorrow the rain will be over, the sun will be shining and the car will start right off.''

"But," Arlene said, "I . . ."

The man's smile was engaging. "Exactly," he said. "I have my car right here. I'll be glad to take you home."

As Arlene hesitated, he added, "That is, if it isn't too far. If it is, I'll see that you get a bus or a cab."

Arlene took another long look at the face. The mouth was smiling. He had regular, even teeth. There was just the hint of something about the lips which indicated he was rather spoiled, but the eyes were expressive and there was a lean competence about him. Moreover, he wouldn't have been in the parking lot unless he was connected with the company, and if he was connected with the executive branch of the company he undoubtedly was all right.

"You're sure I won't be inconveniencing you?"

"Not at all," the man said, opening the door. "Roll up your window tight because it may rain some more tonight. I think it'll be clearing by midnight—at least that's the weather report. Here's my car, right over here."

When she saw the car she knew who he was. This was the son of old Jarvis P. Lamont, the owner of the company—Loring Lamont. He had been away on a tour of South America "surveying the business field" and had only recently returned. Arlene had, however, seen his car once when the elder Lamont had been chauffeured to the plant in it.

The young man held the door open for her with deferential courtesy. As she leaned back against the soft cushions, appreciating the rich leather upholstery, Loring Lamont jumped in the other side, and the motor, already running, purred into multi-cylindered response. A current of warm air flowed reassuringly about her chilled ankles. The big car glided into motion so gently she hardly realized it had started. Loring Lamont drove out past the watchman at the entrance to the parking lot.

"Right or left?" he asked.

"Left," she said.

"That's fine. That's the way I was going. How far?"

"My speedometer clocks it at two miles," she told him. And then added with a nervous laugh, "However, my car is not *quite* as late a model as this one."

"What's the address?" he asked.

She told him.

He frowned, said, "Say, look, I . . . what's your name?"

"Arlene Ferris."

"Mine's Lamont," he said. "Loring Lamont. Look, Miss Ferris, I suddenly remembered I've got some papers to deliver for the old man . . . gosh, I'm sorry. I heard your motor grinding away and realized you were running your battery down, and . . . well, you're pretty easy on the eyes and I guess I forgot my responsibilities for a minute."

"That's all right," she told him. "You can take me to where I can get a bus . . . or a cab."

"Now look," he said, "I can do better than that. If you aren't in a hurry, just settle back and relax. I'll have to deliver those papers, but the car is warm and comfortable. You can turn on the radio, get the latest news, music or anything you want. Then after I've delivered the papers I'll take you home. Or, if you'd like, we can stop for something to eat. I'm absolutely free after I deliver those confounded papers."

She hesitated for a moment, relaxing in the warm, dry comfort of the car. "All right," she said, "I'm in no hurry. If it won't inconvenience you . . ."

"No, no," he protested quickly. "I've got to come back to town anyway after I deliver the papers."

"Back to town?" she asked quickly. "Is it far?"

"Not with this car," he said. "We'll get out of traffic and hit the freeway. Don't worry. Listen to the radio and . . . and I hope your acceptance includes dinner."

"We'll discuss that a little later," she said. And then, with a quick laugh, added, "After I get to know you better."

"Fair enough," he said.

The plant was within a mile of the freeway. Lamont turned on the freeway, drove for some fifteen minutes, then turned

4

off, purred along a paved road for four or five miles, then turned off on a dirt road that wound its way among hills. They were now entirely out of traffic.

"How much farther is it?" Arlene asked, her voice sharpened with suspicion.

"Only a little way," he said. "We have a little country place up here, and my dad's associate is waiting for the papers there. Dad told him I'd be out."

"Oh," she said, and settled back again. She knew of the existence of the country place.

The dirt road was winding and twisting, a barbed-wire fence on each side. There were *No Trespassing* signs, then the car eased to a stop in front of a locked gate. Loring Lamont opened the gate, then drove along a graveled driveway, past a swimming pool, and finally stopped at a house which had a wide porch running around it, furnished with luxurious outdoor furniture.

"Well, what do you know!" Loring Lamont said. "The guy doesn't seem to be here."

"It's certainly all dark," she said, "and the gate was locked."

"We keep the gate locked, but he has a key," Loring said. "However, the place is dark, all right. You wait here and I'll run in and see if there's a note or something. My gosh, Miss Ferris, I certainly hate to have brought you all the way out here in case . . . but the man *must* be here! He's to meet me here and wait for the papers . . . he's staying here tonight and Dad's coming out later for a conference."

"Perhaps he went to sleep," she said, "and forgot to turn on the lights."

"You wait right here," he said. "I'll run in and see."

"What?"

He left the motor idling, jumped out his side of the car and hurried into the house. She saw lights come on, on the porch, then lights in the interior of the house.

It was almost five minutes before he returned. His manner was apologetic. "Now," he said, "there *are* complications.

"Dad's associate was delayed in town," he said. "He's on his way out here now. I got Dad on the phone and told him

5

I'd leave the papers, but he says I'll have to wait, that those papers are classified and that I must deliver them personally and accept a receipt in person. It won't be long. Come on in and we'll wait. I don't think it will be over a few minutes."

She said, "I'll wait here in the car and . . ."

He laughed. "Don't be so upstage. Anyhow, you can't wait in the car. I'm not too long on gas and I don't want to leave the motor idling. Without the motor running, the heater will be off, and . . . come on in, I've turned up the thermostat and the house will warm quickly. You'll be very comfortable. If you'd like a drink we can fix up something that will put sunshine into the atmosphere."

He removed the keys from the car, then went around to her side of the car and held the door open invitingly, and after a moment's hesitation she gave him her hand, jumped to the ground and followed him into the house.

The interior was furnished with fine old Navaho rugs and mission furniture. It had an atmosphere of quiet luxury.

Loring Lamont crossed over to a sideboard, opened a door disclosing a sparkling array of glasses, opened another door to a compartment containing a stock of liquor.

"A drink while we wait?" he asked.

"No, thanks," she said. And then, looking at her wrist watch and for the first time having a vague feeling of apprehension, said, "I really *must* be getting home."

"Oh, come now," he said. "You're not in that much of a hurry. You're going to have dinner with me. Don't worry. Our man will be here in a few minutes, then all I have to do is give him the papers and we'll be on our way. I'm going to have a little drink. Come on, be sociable."

"Well," she said finally, "I'll take a Martini."

He mixed the drinks with a practiced hand. "Dry?" he asked.

"Rather dry, thank you."

He stirred the cocktails, poured them, handed her a glass, said, "Here's to getting better acquainted," and sipped the drink.

The telephone rang.

He frowned his annoyance, said, "*Now* what is it?" and crossed over to the telephone.

"Yes? Hello," he said.

He was silent for a moment, then said, "Oh, come now. I'm sorry but I've waited just as long as I can . . . where is he now? Where can I meet him? But I tell you, I *can't* wait any longer. I have a very important appointment and there's someone with me who has to . . . but look, Dad . . ."

He said "hello" several times, indicating that he had been cut off, then dropped the receiver into place and came across to frown moodily over the glass at Arlene. "This is the deuce of a note," he said. "That was Dad on the telephone. Old Jarvis P. himself, in one of his worst moods. He's opened up a brand new angle of discussion with this man, and I'm instructed to wait until he gets here. He says it may be as much as an hour."

Loring Lamont seemed genuinely concerned. "I'm terribly sorry," he said. "I got you into this. I should have told you right at the start . . . only I didn't know myself. The man was supposed to be waiting out here. When old Jarvis P. gets in one of those moods that's all there is to it. Finish your drink and I'll see if there is anything to eat in the refrigerator. We can at least have an appetizer."

Before she had a chance to protest, he tossed off the rest of his cocktail, went into the kitchen and she heard him rummaging around, opening the door of the refrigerator, closing it, opening and closing cupboard doors.

He came back and said, "How are you on biscuits?"

He said it so easily and naturally that, for the moment, she lost her suspicion and, emboldened by the warmth generated by her drink, said, "I'm pretty darn good on biscuits."

"Swell," he said. "If you'll make some biscuits, I'll fry some ham and eggs, and we can have dinner right here. I'm sorry I got you into this, but I simply must deliver those papers, and . . . it won't be as good a dinner as we could have had in a restaurant—except for the biscuits, of course. I have an idea *they'll* be out of this world!"

"What do you have?" she asked. "Flour, milk, butter, shortening?"

"Everything," he said, "everything except fresh bread. There's no fresh bread here. There's fresh milk. We also have powdered milk, lots of canned goods, lots of ham, eggs, bacon, sausage, coffee, liquor. We keep the place provisioned because Dad likes to come out here occasionally for a conference, a more intimate type of conference than he can have in the office."

She unbuttoned her jacket, asked, "Where's the handwashing department?"

"Through that other room," he said. "First door to the left. You'll find everything—what do you want out here in the kitchen?"

"An apron mostly," she said.

She washed her hands, returned to the kitchen, and, feeling the effect of the cocktail, really began to enjoy herself. Loring Lamont turned on a hi-fi and the room was filled with music. Arlene mixed the biscuits and permitted herself a few dances with Loring Lamont while they were baking. To her delight, they turned out to be perfect—fluffy, flavorable biscuits which melted in her mouth when she tasted one.

Loring Lamont took a bite and was lavish in his praise.

He broke eggs in the frying pan, put ham on hot plates, lifted the percolator of coffee, smiled at her and said, "Now this is real cozy, real homelike."

At that moment the telephone sounded a strident summons.

Loring Lamont seemed for the moment genuinely surprised, then he excused himself, went to the phone, picked up the instrument, said cautiously, "Hello," then after a moment, "Oh, yes, hello . . . hello. All right. Okay. Now wait a minute, let's not discuss it now. I'm . . . just a minute. Hold on. Okay."

Loring Lamont stepped out of the little alcove which housed the telephone, said to Arlene, "Will you take those eggs off the stove? Then go ahead and start eating—I won't be long. This is just an annoying interruption."

He went back, said into the telephone, "Okay. I'll take it n another line. Just hang on for a minute. Okay."

Loring Lamont left the phone off the hook, hurried back

to another part of the lodge, picked up an extension phone and Arlene could hear a mumbled conversation.

She eased the eggs out of the frying pan to the plates, stood looking at the tempting array of ham, eggs and hot biscuits, thinking that this was homelike indeed, that someone always called on the telephone when hot food was on the table.

Then she heard Loring Lamont hurrying back.

He went to the telephone, picked up the receiver, slammed it into place and came toward her.

"Something serious?" she asked.

He kept on advancing toward her. For a moment she was puzzled. Then he had her in his arms, pulled her to him, kissed her hard on the lips.

She tried to push him away.

She was startled at the change in his face. There was no longer any mask of polite affability. There was savage, primitive passion, and a ruthlessness which frightened her.

Arlene pushed herself far enough back to aim a stinging slap at his face.

His eyes showed anger for a moment, then there was only a mocking smile. "Come on, baby," he said, "don't be a prude. Get off your high horse. We're stuck out here for a while and we may as well make the most of it. After all, I'm not exactly repulsive. At least I don't think I am. For your information, girls who have been nice to me have gone a long way in the company. Dad's private secretary, for instance, got *her* job through me. She was in a stenographic pool, and . . ."

"Well, I don't need to go a long way in the company," she blazed. "And *I* don't have to put up with anything like *your* tactics!"

Suddenly she realized a fatal discrepancy in his earlier remarks.

"You told me," she said, "that the man had already started, that he was on his way out here. Then after that telephone call you said your father was detaining him."

"I was mistaken the first time. They'd told me he'd started out so I wouldn't get too impatient. Then Dad called me and said he was holding him there for further conference."

"You know what I think?" she asked, looking at him contemptuously. "I think you had this thing planned from the very start. I don't think there's anyone coming out here. And, in case you want to know it, the reputation you have among the girls at the office isn't particularly flattering. I understand you think that anyone who works for the company has personal private obligations to you."

"It's an idea," he said, laughing. "Come off your high horse, Arlene. And you aren't going to gain anything, either now or later, by heaping abuse on me. You may as well face realities. Since you want to make something of it, I'll admit that I've been crazy about you ever since I got back from South America and saw you there in the office.

"If you want to know it, I lifted a part of the distributor out of your car so it wouldn't start. I 'happened' along at just the psychological moment. You're entirely correct in assuming that I made up this whole story. When I came in the first time I called a friend of mine and told him to call me back on the phone in exactly seven minutes. That was simply a decoy call.

"Now then, Sweetheart, I have the keys to the car. You're going to stay here until I get good and ready to let you go home. If you don't act up, we're going to have a pleasant evening. If you act up . . . well, that's all the good it's going to do you.

"Come on, Arlene, you may as well yield to the inevitable with good grace."

"It's not inevitable," she said. "I'm not yielding and I don't have any good grace. Now, you take me home at once or I'll lodge a criminal complaint against you, regardless of who you are."

He laughed and said, "Try it. See how far you get. Who do you think is going to believe a story about you coming out here with me, about having a drink with me and all that, and then suddenly becoming upstage?"

He dangled the car keys. "Here they are," he said. "Come and get them. I dare you."

Seething with indignation, she came at him in an avalanche of human fury, and was immediately shoved with brutal strength back through the dining room, into the living room. He pushed her back against a davenport until she collapsed. Then he was once more caressing her passionately.

She doubled her knees, got them against his chest, pressed her back against the davenport and gave a sudden push.

The push broke his hold. He staggered backwards. She was on her feet and picked up a chair. "You . . . you beast!" she said.

He laughed. "I like spitfires," he said. "Come on, baby, you can't get anywhere with this stuff."

She realized that he must have done this many times before, that he knew exactly what he was doing.

"I'm going to have you arrested if you so much as put your hand on me again," she said.

"Let me tell you something about the law in this state," he replied calmly. "I happen to know what it is. If a woman presents a charge for a criminal attack against a man, her own previous moral character can be inquired into. Dad's lawyers even gave me the California case that determined the point. It's People vs. Battilana. That means that with all the money at my command, I can put detectives on your back trail. I can turn you inside out on the witness stand. I can ask you names, dates, specific occasions, and . . ."

In an ecstasy of blind fury, she flung the chair.

He was hardly expecting this maneuver. The chair caught him low in the abdomen. For a moment there was a look of utter surprise on his face, then he doubled over in pain.

Arlene made for the door.

She grabbed her raincoat as she went through the reception hallway, then she was out on the porch, running down the gravel driveway, past the swimming pool, out to the dirt road.

She knew that he had the keys to the car, that it was no use to try and get transportation until she came to the main traveled highway, and even then it was doubtful if any cars would be along.

She didn't bother to put on the raincoat but held it bundled under her left arm. She ran pell-mell down the road until she found herself getting short of breath. Then she slowed to a walk and looked back over her shoulder.

She could see a blob of light from the house, then she saw a moving pencil of light, the beam of the headlights swinging around the driveway. Soon the headlights would be illuminating the road, cutting through the moist darkness.

She swung abruptly from the road, came to the barbed-wire fence, and crawled through. Then she hesitated a moment and turned back toward the house, keeping in the shadows cast by the trees.

The twin beams of the headlights swept down the road. The car was coming, but it was coming so slowly that for a moment she was completely fooled.

She stood there, protected by the trunk of an oak, watching the creeping lights moving slowly along the road.

The car came to the exact place where she had detoured to crawl through the fence and stopped.

Then as she saw Loring Lamont getting out of the car and walking to the front of the headlights, she saw the beam of a flashlight playing along the ground. The light switched abruptly and came toward the fence.

For the first time she realized the reason the car had been going so slowly. Lamont had known that she couldn't keep up a running pace down the mile or so of country road which was fenced on both sides. He had been following her tracks in the wet dirt, and when he came to the place where she had turned off, he was using the flashlight to track her.

For a moment she was cold with fear. This man knew exactly what he was doing. He was cold, ruthless and determined.

The beam of the flashlight following her tracks came to the fence.

Arlene Ferris wanted to scream and run, then suddenly her brain began to function smoothly. She moved quietly along the fence, then again crawled through the barbed wire and down into the roadway.

Lamont had come to the place now where she had been standing. It was a little more difficult tracking her in the terrain which had not been cleared into a roadway. But, nev-

12

ertheless, he was following her steps. Her heels made unmistakable marks in the soft ground.

Loring Lamont had made one fatal error. He had left the headlights on, the motor running, the key in the ignition lock.

When she was within six or eight feet of the car, Lamont came to the place where she had gone through the fence for the second time. He evidently realized then what she had in mind.

The questing finger of the flashlight darted along the road, then suddenly caught her in its brilliance.

There was momentary panic in his voice. "You touch that car and you'll go to jail!" he shouted. Then he was scrambling through the fence, trying to get to the road in time to overtake her.

She jumped into the car, threw up her wet skirt in order to give her legs plenty of freedom, pushed the driving control lever and felt the car glide into motion.

He was in the roadway right behind her now. She could see the flashlight in the rearview mirror. Her toe found the throttle. She pressed down and the car leaped ahead as though it had been propelled by a rocket.

Surprised at the swift acceleration, she almost went into the ditch at the first turn. But she finally got control of the car. The power steering was new to her and bothered her for the first two hundred yards. After that, she had the car fairly well mastered, and by the time she had turned into the main highway she was handling the wheel like a veteran.

She drove to her apartment, left the car parked there, jumped into dry clothes, then, actuated by a bit of sardonic humor, looked up Loring Lamont's address in the telephone directory, drove the car to his apartment house, parked it in the street directly in front of a fireplug, walked four blocks to the main boulevard where there was a drugstore, phoned for a taxicab and went home.

Chapter 2

The next day was bright and sunny, as Loring Lamont had predicted. Arlene Ferris had a repairman look at her car. Sure enough, he reported that a part had been taken from the electrical distributor. A new part was found and put into place, and the car ran perfectly.

Arlene typed mechanically, awaiting the summons which would bring her to the office of the office manager. She was grimly determined that this was one time Loring Lamont, spoiled son of a rich and powerful father, was not going to get away with it. Let them try to fire her. She'd show them she wasn't a chattel.

During the first part of the morning she debated whether or not to prosecute.

They would, of course, put detectives at work digging up every event in her past life. They would get the names of every boy with whom she had gone out. Every petting party would be turned into a major indiscretion. They would attempt to blacken her character, would doubtless claim that she had tried blackmail.

She knew that, for her own sake, it would be better to keep quiet, to say nothing. But she also felt that too many young women in Loring Lamont's life had decided to follow the line of least resistance, thereby making it doubly hard for the next young woman on whom Loring Lamont cast his predatory eyes.

Shortly before noon she made up her mind. She went to the women's lounge, looked up the telephone number of Perry Mason, attorney at law, and called his office.

Eventually she was connected with Della Street, Perry Mason's secretary.

"This is Arlene Ferris," she said. "I'm working at the

Lamont Rolling, Casting and Engineering Company. I get off work at five o'clock. Would it be possible for me to see Mr. Mason tonight on a personal and very important matter? I can get away earlier, if it's necessary."

"Just a moment," Della Street said.

She was back on the line within a few minutes. "Do you think you could get excused so as to be here at two-thirty?" she asked.

"I'll be there," Arlene Ferris promised.

She felt as if a load had been lifted from her mind. She was going to go through with it. She'd show Loring Lamont she wasn't going to put up with that sort of treatment.

At one-thirty there was a ripple of excitement in the office. Jarvis P. Lamont, looking as though the world had caved in on him, hurried from the office. The second vice president emerged to run after Lamont.

There had been no sign of Loring Lamont.

A few minutes before two, Arlene Ferris went to the office manager. "I worked late last night," she said, "and now I have to be out for about an hour. You can dock me if you wish."

George Albert seemed somewhat nonplussed. "This is a *most* unusual request, Miss Ferris," he said.

"I know," Arlene said, "but it's an unusual situation."

"Well," he replied, hesitating, "of course, we are aware of the fact that you *have* put in overtime—I guess it's all right. You understand, Miss Ferris, the problem is that of creating a precedent—it sometimes happens that girls have dental or doctor appointments where they *have* to be excused, but if we are too liberal they'll be making beauty parlor appointments and we can't tell where things will stop."

"I understand," Arlene said briefly, and paused.

"Very well," Albert agreed reluctantly. "We'll expect you back in an hour."

"An hour and a half," Arlene said, firmly.

The man seemed puzzled by Arlene's manner. "Very well, Miss Ferris," he said, and let it go at that.

Arlene made no attempt to take her car, but took a cab so she wouldn't have to waste time finding a parking place. She wanted to get back within the designated period of an hour and a half because she had said she would, but she felt it really didn't make much difference. After all, she was quite certain that by this time tomorrow she would no longer be an employee of the company.

Chapter 3

As Arlene Ferris finished her story, Della Street, Perry Mason's confidential secretary, looked up from her notebook. Her eyes were sympathetic as she waited for the lawyer's decision.

Mason, his face granite hard, his eyes shrewdly appraising the young woman, said, "Exactly what do you want to do, Miss Ferris?"

"I . . . I want to show him that women aren't chattels, that a working girl is entitled to consideration—just because I work for a company as a stenographer doesn't mean that I automatically have to become the plaything of the spoiled son of the owner of the business."

"You want to teach him a lesson, is that it?" Mason asked.

"Not exactly. I don't want to have to live my life feeling that women who work for an organization are . . . oh, all right, I *do* want to teach him a lesson."

"How?"

"That's what I wanted you to tell me."

"You can file a suit for damages," Mason said, "or you can go to the police and lodge a criminal complaint. But you can't do both."

"Why?"

"For practical reasons. The minute you file a suit for damages, the criminal case goes out the window. A shrewd defense attorney would make it appear that you were trying to capitalize on the experience."

"I see—and what if I file a suit and don't make a complaint to the police?"

"There, of course," Mason said, "you get to the ultimate question of what a jury will do, and, again, that depends on

17

exactly what you want. If you want money to salve your injured feelings . . ."

"I don't. I just want to . . . it's hard to explain. I want to stand up for my rights. I want to stand up for my sex."

Mason nodded. "I think you measure up," he said. "If you want to put a stop to this sort of thing, we'll put a stop to it—but it isn't going to be easy. They'll throw mud, they'll claim blackmail, they'll have young Lamont testifying that you deliberately led him on, that *you* were the one who made passes at *him*, that when he was too bored to acquiesce you ran true to the old adage that hell hath no fury like a woman scorned."

Her face went suddenly white. "He'd do that?"

"Sure, he'd do that," Mason said. "You don't expect a man of that type to tell the truth, do you? Do you still want to go ahead with it?"

"Mr. Mason," she said, "I'll fight this thing through—if you'll stay with me I'll stay with the case. Once I start fighting I keep on fighting."

"Good girl," Mason told her.

He turned to Della Street. "Ring Paul Drake at the Drake Detective Agency. Ask him if he can come down here right away. Let's start getting evidence before young Lamont begins to realize what he's up against."

Mason turned to Arlene Ferris. "You say you left his car in front of a fireplug?"

"I parked it right smack-dab in front of a fireplug. I just hope they give him a dozen tickets for illegal parking."

Mason smiled, said, "That probably gives us our chance. He'll be making excuses for the illegal parking, and it will be interesting to see what story he tells."

"You don't think he'll tell the truth, do you?"

"No," Mason said, "I don't. But I do think that he'll tell a story to the effect that some angry girl was trying to get even with him. It may well differ from the story he'll tell when he gets into court.

"By the time he gets into court you will be described as the aggressor. You will have been literally throwing yourself at him, trying to advance yourself in the company by courting

18

his favor. You say that he told you some other woman had got ahead through him?"

"Yes. The private secretary to Jarvis P. Lamont."

"Would you know her name?"

"Edith Bristol," she said.

"Have you met her?"

"I've seen her a number of times."

"Can you describe her?"

"A very good-looking girl—twenty-six or twenty-seven, really an outstanding figure, and . . . well, she'd stand out anywhere as a real beauty if it wasn't . . ."

"If it wasn't for what?" Mason asked.

"Her eyes," she said. "There's something about them, a defeated look . . . it's hard to describe. I never thought of it before, but now that you mention her in connection with . . ."

Paul Drake's code knock sounded on the door.

"That's Paul Drake," Mason said to Della Street. "Let him in."

By way of explanation, Mason said to Arlene Ferris, "The Drake Detective Agency does all of my investigative work. They have offices on the same floor here in the building. You'll like Paul Drake. He seems rather casual when you first meet him, but I can assure you he's thoroughly competent."

Della Street opened the door. Mason said, "Miss Ferris, this is Paul Drake, head of the Drake Detective Agency. Sit down, Paul."

Paul Drake acknowledged the introduction, seated himself across from Mason's desk.

Mason said, "Are you acquainted with the Lamont family, Paul? The Rolling, Casting and Engineering Company?"

Drake's eyes narrowed. "What about them, Perry?"

Mason said, "They have a country place up toward the hills—a real country lodge, I guess you'd call it, complete with swimming pool, Navaho rugs, barbecue, liquor closet, and the rest of it."

Drake nodded. "I know where it is."

"Loring Lamont's car was parked in front of a fireplug

19

last night," Mason said. "I'd like to know what time it was moved and by whom. I'd like to know what Loring Lamont has to say about how it happened to be parked there, whether he accepts or disclaims responsibility, and, if possible, I'd like to find who some of his friends are, people in whom he would confide. I want to see if he has talked about where he was last night. I want to find out about all this before he knows any investigation is being made."

Drake's eyes met Mason's steadily. "Miss Ferris is the client?" he asked.

Mason nodded.

Drake said, "I hate to do this, Perry. Probably I should get you to one side, but it may be that on account of the time element involved we don't have that much time to waste. Loring Lamont was murdered last night."

Mason's eyes snapped wide open. Arlene Ferris gave a dismayed gasp.

"Go on," Mason said, his face hard with expressionless concentration.

"I don't know too much about it," Drake said. "I heard a news broadcast over the radio. I was interested in developments in another case that we're working on, and I thought the police might have released some news this afternoon, so I tuned in on a broadcast about fifteen minutes before you called. All I heard was the bare announcement that Loring Lamont, son of Jarvis P. Lamont, the famed industrialist, had been murdered last night. His body was discovered in the rustic retreat maintained by the company as a place of recreation and for conferences. He had been stabbed in the back with a butcher knife."

"Any clues?" Mason asked.

"That was all the radio report said."

"Any statement about the guilty person?"

"Police were trying to find a young woman who had apparently been with him last night," Drake said.

Mason said, "All right, Paul, beat it."

Drake said, "Perhaps I . . ."

Mason interrupted. "Time is precious, Paul. I've got to give some advice to my client. I've got to give it to her fast.

20

It has to be confidential. If you're here there's no privilege in connection with the communication. Conversations between an attorney and his client are privileged, provided he doesn't have outsiders present. Della Street isn't an outsider. She's included in the legal privilege. Get going.''

Drake was out of the chair in one swift motion. He jerked open the door, smiled at Arlene Ferris, said, ''You couldn't be in better hands,'' and shot out into the corridor.

Mason said, ''All right now, let's get it fast. Did you kill him?''

She shook her head.

''What time was it when you left there?''

''I don't know. Perhaps—well, somewhere around seven o'clock.''

''And you got your clothes pretty muddy?''

She nodded.

''Your clothes were torn?''

''My blouse was torn.''

''Bra?'' Mason asked.

''I was generally mussed up. I had to make emergency repairs after I got out on the main highway.''

''You drove his car?''

She nodded.

''And you parked it directly in front of a fireplug?''

Again she nodded.

''The rearview mirror is the most sensitive place on a car for fingerprints.'' Mason said. ''A person adjusting a rearview mirror will almost invariably leave prints of the third and fourth fingers. Do you remember if you adjusted the mirror? You must have if you were using it in driving.''

''I adjusted it,'' she admitted.

''Gloves?''

''No.''

Mason said, ''Listen very, very carefully to what I have to say. Flight is an evidence of guilt. Failure to report a crime may also become a crime. On the other hand, a person is entitled to follow the advice of an attorney. If the attorney gives wrong advice that's his responsibility. If he advises a client to do something illegal he is subject to disbarment. Do you understand?"

She nodded.

"All right," Mason said. "I do *not* want you to resort to flight. Do you understand?"

She nodded.

"On the other hand, I don't dare have you tell your story to the police right at the present time. We'll need to get it corroborated with some sort of evidence. You took off your torn clothes and left them in your apartment?"

She nodded.

"They're in your apartment now?"

"Yes."

"What about your outer garments?"

"I got mud on my skirt when I crawled through the barbed-wire fence."

"Now, think carefully," Mason said. "Were there any bloodstains?"

She hesitated for a moment, then wordlessly pulled up her skirt. On the thigh of her right leg was a long, red scratch. "I did that," she said, "when I plunged through the fence the second time—I was in a hurry. I wanted to get to his car before he realized that he'd left himself in a vulnerable position. As soon as I heard the sound of the idling motor I knew that if I could get to his car first . . . well, I guess I always do think in terms of a counteroffensive. I did *so* want to turn the tables on him. I threw discretion to the winds. I just shot under that fence and that's where I got the scratch."

"And it bled?"

"It bled."

"On the skirt?"

She nodded.

"The skirt was torn?" Mason asked.

"I don't think it was," she said. "I shot through under the fence feet first. My skirt was way up around my middle somewhere. My . . . my panties were stained from the mud. There was mud on the skirt."

"You washed your undergarment?" Mason asked.

22

She shook her head and said, "I left everything in my laundry basket."

"All right," Mason said, "we've got to concede certain trumps to the police. They're bound to take some tricks. Give me the key to your apartment. Authorize me to go there and do anything I see fit."

She opened her purse, handed him a key.

"Are you going to remove my clothes?"

"Heavens no! That would be tampering with evidence. I'm going to let the police do all the tampering with the evidence."

"I'm afraid I don't understand," she said.

"I don't want you to," Mason told her. "Now I want just as much time as I can get before you are questioned by the police. You'll have to co-operate on that."

"But I thought you told me you didn't want me to resort to flight."

"I don't," Mason said. "I want you to do exactly what any other young woman would do under the circumstances."

"What do you mean?" she asked. "Wouldn't it be normal to go to the police?"

"You're following *my* advice," Mason told her. "*I* will tell the police everything I feel that they need to know, at the time I think they should know it. Right at the moment I want you out of circulation, but I *don't* want you to resort to flight— now there's a difference. Do you understand?"

"I'm not certain that I do."

Mason said, "Do exactly as I tell you. If it comes to a showdown and you are absolutely forced to account for your actions, you can state you were following my advice. But I don't want you to make that statement until I tell you to.

"Now then, the first thing is to get yourself fired."

"That won't be difficult," she said. "Once it becomes known that I . . . ."

Mason shook his head. "With Loring Lamont dead, there is no way that it's going to become known unless you left some evidence on the ground linking you to that country lodge."

"And if there isn't any such evidence?"

"They may not know that you were out there with him for some time," Mason said, "but we can't count on that. They may be looking for you any minute now. The first thing you've got to do is to get fired. Go back to your job and get discharged—at once."

She was thoughtful. "It might not be easy to . . ."

"I don't care whether it's easy or not," Mason snapped. "Get yourself fired."

"Then what?" she asked.

Mason said, "You have a girl friend somewhere here in the city?"

"Not right in the city."

"Close by?"

"Santa Monica."

"What's her name?"

"Madge Elwood."

"How old?"

"Twenty-seven."

"Blonde or brunette?"

"Brunette."

"What does she look like?"

"She's about my size. She has a wonderful figure. She was selected as a beauty queen a few years ago. I'm not as good-looking as she is, but there is quite a remarkable resemblance. Some people think we are related."

"What does she do now?"

"She's a secretary."

"Good job?" Mason asked.

"Yes. It's a responsible position."

"You've known her since you came here?"

"Long before that. We've been friends for years. It was through her that I came here—it was, in fact, through her that I got this job at the Lamont Company. She had some contact there, I don't know just who it was, but I know that she put through a telephone call and then told me to go in and things certainly were made easy for me. I just breezed into a position while some of the other applicants were still sitting around waiting."

Mason nodded. "Go get yourself fired. Then ring up

24

Madge Elwood. Tell her that you've lost your job and that you just *have* to see her. Go down and stay with her in Santa Monica. Stay there overnight.''

"And what do I tell her?"

"Tell her you got fired. Tell her you're satisfied you were discharged because Loring Lamont made a report to the boss, that he made a pass at you and you turned him down. Don't tell your friend any of the details. Simply say you're too upset to talk about it.''

"She already knows about the trouble I had with Loring Lamont," Arlene said. "You see, since I got the job through her, I felt I owed her an explanation. I rang her up last night as soon as I got back and asked her why she hadn't warned me about the wolves in the company.''

"And what did she say?" Mason asked.

She hesitated. "Madge is a good sport. Of course she's had people make passes at her. We all have. I guess it's just a question of how you handle them . . . I suppose I could have handled the situation last night if it hadn't been . . . well, he got this last telephone call and it seemed to do things to him. He just flung all tact and discretion to the winds . . . Well, you wanted to know about Madge . . . she asked me if I thought there were any jobs where the boss wouldn't make an occasional pass, so I described what happened— and when I told her about leaving his car in front of the fireplug I thought she'd die laughing.''

Mason was thoughtful. "You'd better run down to visit your friend," he said. "Leave her telephone number and address with Miss Street here. And when Madge hears about the murder, tell her to keep quiet about everything you told her, and . . .''

"I'm not to tell her about the murder?"

"Not a word—not a word about that to anyone.''

"Suppose she comes right out and asks me?"

"She won't," Mason said. "When you tell a friend about having a struggle with some man, the friend doesn't say, 'Oh, is he still alive?' Can you depend on this Madge Elwood?"

"Heavens, yes. She's a wonderful friend, very loyal.''

"Get started," Mason said.

"But I'll need my key to go to my apartment and get . . ."

"You *don't* go to your apartment," Mason said. "You don't get a thing."

"Not even the clothes that . . ."

"There isn't that much time. Call up Madge Elwood as soon as you get yourself fired. Now leave her address and phone number with Miss Street and get started."

Chapter 4

It was five-forty when Paul Drake's code knock sounded on the exit door of the private office.

Mason nodded to Della Street, who opened the door.

"Hi, Della," Paul said, and nodded to Mason. "You want the latest on this Lamont murder?"

"What have you got, Paul?"

"Now, mind you, Perry, I don't know what you know, and I don't want to know what you know. I don't want to take that responsibility."

Mason nodded.

"I'm telling you what *I* know," Drake said.

"Go ahead."

"This rolling, casting and engineering company does some classified work. Not too much, but some. They have the place guarded. You need a clearance in order to get in. They have an executive parking lot reserved for people in the engineering office. There's a little cubbyhole office and a man stays on duty there. It's his job to see that cars that go in or out have the sticker of the company on them and are driven by authorized personnel. Actually, he doesn't pay too much attention to the cars going *out*, but the cars going *in* are different. He looks over the car and the driver. If he doesn't recognize the driver, or the car isn't properly fixed up with a sticker, he stops the car and makes a detailed check.

"He remembers that last night, about quarter to six, he saw Loring Lamont driving out. There was a young woman in the car with Loring. He's given the police a description of the woman. So far, it's more or less a general description—dark hair, rather young, somewhere in the twenties, good-looking. The police are acting on the theory that Loring Lamont had a date and went out to this country

27

place the company maintains in the hills west of the city, that they had a drink, that Lamont cooked up a supper of ham and eggs, and that after supper there was an argument and the girl stabbed him.

"The police aren't releasing anything to the public as yet, but of course they're very anxious to find this girl and question her.

"The general gossip is that Lamont was inclined to be impulsive, as far as women were concerned."

Mason digested the information.

"I don't want to make any suggestions," Drake said, "but since the young woman was seen leaving the parking lot with Loring Lamont, the police have an idea that she was some woman who worked in the place. Since Lamont's car went out about five-forty-five, they have the idea that she was probably an employee who may have been working late, that Lamont had a date with her to go out after hours and had waited for her.

"You give the police that much to work with and it won't be long before they come up with an answer—now if that answer is going to involve your client, it's going to be a whole lot better to have her come out with her story first and claim that she was protecting herself against attack. If she waits until after the police pick her up, then it isn't going to look so good."

"She stabbed him in the back in self-defense, eh?" Mason asked.

"It *could* have happened," Drake said.

"Thanks a lot," Mason told him. "Keep your men on the job. Just where is this place, Paul?"

Drake took a map from his pocket. "Here's an automobile map, and here's a large-scale sketch map showing just how you get to the place. I understand the police are still out there, so don't let our mutual friend, Lieutenant Tragg, catch you snooping around or he'll immediately put another two and two together. I understand he's working on the job at the special request of Jarvis P. Lamont, who, as it happens, has a hell of a lot of influence."

Mason nodded, took the map, said, "Keep on the job,

Paul. Della and I had planned to go out for dinner, and I was going to get in touch with you after dinner. As it is, we'll probably wait here a little while. I'm going to have to think this thing out."

Drake left the office. Della Street glanced apprehensively at Perry Mason.

Mason looked at his wrist watch. "Give them a couple of hours," he said, "and they'll have the answer."

"And then?" she asked.

"Then," Mason said, "they'll be looking for Arlene Ferris, and . . . Della, you have that Santa Monica number?"

Della street nodded.

"Put through a call," Mason said.

"Ask for Arlene Ferris?"

"Heavens, no!" Mason said. "Ask for Madge Elwood."

Della Street gave him a quick glance, put through the call. A moment later she said, "Miss Elwood on the line."

Mason picked up the telephone. "Madge Elwood?"

"Yes."

"I'm Perry Mason, the lawyer, but please don't mention my name at your end of the line. Have you talked with Arlene Ferris?"

"Why yes . . . but good heavens! You! I'm a fan of yours . . . I . . . well, I'll hold it."

"Is Arlene there?"

"Yes."

"I want you to do something."

"Yes. What?"

"Confine yourself to noncommittal answers," Mason said, "that won't let Arlene Ferris know who is talking. I want you to do something that is for her best interests, but she may not approve of what I'm going to do."

"Very well."

"Are you willing to help?"

"Anything."

"Do you have a car?"

"Yes."

"You know where Arlene Ferris has her apartment?"

"Of course."

Mason said, "Make some excuse to Arlene. Tell her that you have a date with a boy friend, tell her to stay there in your apartment and not to go out until you get back."

"And then?"

"Then get in your car and drive at once to Arlene Ferris' apartment. Park your car about a block away—do you smoke?"

"Yes. Why?"

"When you get in front of the apartment house," Mason said, "light a cigarette."

"Isn't that rather—unusual?"

"You mean you don't smoke on the street?"

"Something like that."

"That's why I want you to do something that will tell me who you are. It has to be unusual but not suspiciously so. Light a cigarette when you're right in front of the apartment house."

"Yes. Go on."

"Now then," Mason said, "after you've struck the match and lit your cigarette, stand there for a minute. If the coast is clear, I'll come up to you. If I don't come up and speak to you within a matter of two or three seconds, just keep right on walking past the apartment house. Walk around the block, get into your car, drive back to Santa Monica and forget about the whole thing. Have you got that straight?"

"I think so."

"All right," Mason said. "How long will it take you to get there?"

"I can make it in . . . oh, I'd say twenty-five minutes from now."

"All right," Mason told her. "I'll be waiting. Remember, if I don't get in touch with you shortly after you've lit the cigarette, keep right on walking. Don't look at the apartment house or look around. Just walk on by as though you had stopped to light a cigarette and that was all. Get started now. That's a good girl."

Mason hung up.

Della Street raised her eyebrows in silent interrogation.

"I'm sorry," Mason said, "but you're going to have to

wait this one out, Della. Stand by the telephone. Wait for me. Get me my miniature camera and the flash gun. I'll probably want some pictures. Get our photographer to stay on in his studio.''

"How long will you be gone?" she asked.

"I don't know. I'm going to try to turn a red herring into a decoy.''

"I'll wait," Della Street told him.

"Good girl," he said.

He went to his car, drove to a place where he could find a parking place within a couple of blocks of the building where Arlene Ferris had her apartment, smoked a cigarette, then took the camera case from the car and went to stand unobtrusively in the shadows in front of the building.

A few minutes later a young woman walking briskly along the sidewalk paused directly in front of the apartment house, took a cigarette from her purse, scraped a match into flame and held a light in her cupped hands.

She did a good job of acting, letting the match blow out, fumbling for another match, taking time to light the cigarette the second time.

Mason stepped up. "Madge Elwood?"

"Mr. Mason?"

"Yes. Let's go."

"Where?"

"At the moment, to Arlene Ferris' apartment. You're willing to help?"

"Heavens, yes! I'm willing to do everything I can. But will you tell me what this is all about, Mr. Mason? I had the news turned on, on the radio driving in, and I heard that Loring Lamont, son of Jarvis P. Lamont, had been killed. I knew that Arlene had been forced to fight him off . . . tell me, is there any . . . any possible connection?"

"You said you wanted to help Arlene?" Mason interrupted.

"I do."

"All right then," Mason said. "Come on up to Arlene's apartment.''

"You haven't answered my question, Mr. Mason."

"That's a very interesting observation on your part, and it's entirely accurate," Mason said. "I haven't. Come on, let's go."

They entered the apartment house, took the elevator to the fourth floor, and Mason said, "You know where Arlene's apartment is?"

"Yes, of course."

"Lead the way," Mason said. "Take this key. Open the door casually."

She looked at him questioningly, then took the key which he handed her, walked down the corridor, opened the door, went in, switched on the lights and held the door open for Mason.

"All right," she said, closing the door behind them. "Now what?"

Mason said, "You're going to have to take me on trust."

"I've done that long ago."

"Arlene says you're a good friend of hers."

"I am."

"That you're loyal to your friends."

"I try to be."

"How long have you known her?"

"Seven years."

"You knew her before she came here?"

"Yes. We were together in the East, and then I came out here and we didn't see each other for a couple of years—but we kept up a correspondence. Arlene is a wonderful girl. She'd do anything for me and I think I'd do anything for her."

Mason said, "You look very much like her. There's a striking resemblance."

"Isn't it weird? People always take us for sisters. Sometimes they get us mixed up; yet, as far as we can tell, there isn't any relationship."

Mason sized up the young woman, eying her speculatively until Madge stirred uneasily.

"Don't look at me like that. I feel you're mentally . . ."

"I am, but not the way you think. Where does Arlene keep her clothes?"

"In this closet."

32

"Find something you can wear," Mason said. "Go in the bathroom and put it on. Take off that skirt and give it to me."

"And then?" she asked.

Mason said, "Then, in case you are questioned, you are to say nothing—absolutely nothing. In the meantime, hold still, I want some pictures."

Mason took out the camera, focused it, took several snapshots, said, "Okay, now go change."

Madge Elwood hesitated. "Are you certain you know what you want? Perhaps I know some things you don't know, Mr. Mason."

"Look, we haven't time for a debate. Are you willing to help Arlene?"

"Yes."

"You buy your clothes in Santa Monica?"

"Yes."

"Your skirt has a Santa Monica label?"

"Yes."

Mason walked over to the window of the apartment, looking down at the street. Madge Elwood still hesitated, studying him thoughtfully.

Mason saw a police car glide around the corner, come to a stop in front of the building.

Mason whirled. "All right," he said, "it's too late. You haven't time to do it now. The police are here. Come on, we've got to go."

"This would help Arlene?" she asked.

"I think it would have helped. It's too late now."

She reached an instant decision, unfastened the belt on the skirt, pulled a zipper, dropped it to the floor and stepped out, clad in stockings and panties. "Throw me that skirt. The one on the first hanger," she said.

Mason shook his head. "I tell you there isn't time."

"Throw it, damn it!" she said. "I'll dress in the hall."

Mason looked at her long, graceful legs, said, "You'd start a riot, but . . ." He grabbed the skirt off the first hanger. "Okay, we'll try it. Whip into that skirt. Quick!"

While Madge Elwood was dropping the skirt over her head, Mason took out his pocketknife, made a cut in the skirt

33

Madge Elwood had taken off, and ripped out a piece of the garment from the hem.

Madge Elwood, holding the skirt about her with one hand, pulled open the door.

"This way," Mason said.

They raced down the corridor to the stair door and were opening it just as the elevator came to a stop. Lt. Tragg and a plain-clothes officer stepped out into the corridor as the door slid shut behind Mason and Madge Elwood.

Madge Elwood twisted her hips into the skirt, hitched it around, pulled up the zipper, said, "Now what?"

"Now," Mason said, "we go down two flights, sit on the stairs and wait."

"And if one of the tenants uses the stairs?"

"We are engaged in low-voiced conversation," Mason said. "I am telling you that my divorce decree won't be final for another three months. You are telling me that if I am not in a position to marry you, you're going to break the whole thing off, that you're tired of being kept dangling on a string, that we can't go on living like this."

"It seems to me," she said, smiling, "that I've read the lines somewhere. I may even have heard them."

"You might have," Mason said dryly. "How are you on acting?"

"We can try. And how long do we keep it up?"

"Thirty minutes anyway," Mason said. "Perhaps longer. We'll light a dozen cigarettes simultaneously and let them burn until they get down to stubs so we can have evidence that the conversation has been going for some time."

"I'm in your hands," she told him. "In your position you have to know what you're doing, and it has to be legal."

"Sometimes," Mason admitted, "I wish I had a greater margin of safety, but . . . well, I can tell you this much. I try to give a client all the breaks. There's a popular belief that circumstantial evidence leads to injustices. Actually, circumstantial evidence is some of the best evidence we have, *if* it is properly interpreted.

"The evidence that is really responsible for more miscar-
34

riages of justice than anything else is personal identification."

"And I take it this has to do with personal identification?"

"It does," Mason said. "I have reason to believe that a certain witness is going to identify anyone the officers point out to him as being the person he saw in a certain car with a certain party."

"How interesting. Don't you have the right to cross-examine such a person?"

"Sure, I have the *right*," Mason said, "and how much good does it do? According to my theory, you can cross-examine a man by putting him in a situation where his actions contradict his words a whole lot better than you can by trying to get his words to contradict his words."

"That," she said, "sounds very lawyer-like and very Perry Mason-like, if you don't mind my saying so. Shall we go down another flight of stairs and engage in our act?"

Mason nodded.

They walked down the stairs to the flight between the second and third floors. There Madge Elwood gathered her borrowed skirt tightly around her and made room for Mason to sit close to her.

Mason lit one cigarette after another, left them burning on the stairs until they got down to stubs, then ground them out.

"It really looks as though we've been here a long time," she said.

"I hope so," Mason told her.

"The arm, Mr. Mason."

"What about the arm?"

"It's out of place."

She gently took his left arm and put it around her waist. "Now then," she said, "I'll put my head on your shoulder and in this trusting, intimate position I'll ask you if you've read any good books lately."

"I don't have time to read," Mason said. "I keep too damned busy."

"It sounds like an interesting life," she murmured seductively.

"It is."

"I've followed your adventures, if that's the proper word, in the newspapers. You certainly seem to handle your cases in a spectacular way."

"I try to make them interesting," Mason said. "Jurors are human. They'll pay attention to something that interests them. If you start droning through the usual routine of handling a case they'll lose interest and you'll lose the case."

"You mean your client will," she muttered dreamily.

"With me it's the same thing," Mason said.

"With some lawyers it isn't," she told him, and snuggled closer.

Half an hour later Mason sighed, said, "This has been a perfectly delightful thirty minutes. Now run down to the door to the second floor, take the elevator down from there. Go through the lobby and walk out. If there's a police car at the curb, just keep on going. Don't come back. If the police car is gone, pretend that you forgot something, come running back to the elevator, take it to the second floor, then come to the stair door and beckon to me."

"If the police car's there, I'm to keep right on going?"

"Yes."

"Going where?"

"To Santa Monica."

"When will I see you again?"

"I don't know, but get tomorrow off if you can so you will be available for a phone call."

"On my way," she said.

Mason helped her to her feet. She took out Arlene Ferris' skirt, tripped lightly down the stairs and through the stair door.

She did not return.

Mason sat there for another twenty minutes. His extravagant buildup with the cigarettes had consumed the entire supply in his cigarette case and he looked at his watch a dozen times in the last ten minutes of his wait. Then finally he arose, squared his shoulders, dusted off his clothes, walked down the stairs to the second floor, took the elevator to the lobby and walked out through the door.

The police car was no longer at the curb.

Mason walked to the place where he had parked his car and drove to his office building.

Chapter 5

Mason latchkeyed the door of his office.

Della Street had set up the electric percolator. The aroma of freshly brewed coffee filled the office.

"Smells good," Mason said. "How about a cup?"

"I made it for you," she said. "How did you come out?"

"Yes and no," Mason told her. "The police are on the trail of Arlene Ferris. They've got that far."

He took from his pocket the fragment he had cut from the hem of the skirt Madge Elwood had been wearing.

"What's that?"

Mason grinned and said, "I refuse to answer on the ground that it might incriminate me. Are you hungry?"

"I'm absolutely starved."

"All right," he said. "We have about an hour's nefarious activity to engage in, then we are going to eat."

"We can't eat first?"

Mason shook his head. "It's too close . . . heard anything from Paul?"

"Nothing more."

"Give him a ring," Mason said. "See if there's anything new. Tell him we'll call him again later on in the evening."

Della Street dialed Drake's office, conveyed the message to the detective, put on her hat and coat.

"Do you have an extra pair of shoes in the office?" Mason asked.

"Yes. Why?"

"You're going to get those pretty muddy."

"I have a pair of rather flat heels and some higher heels."

"Wear the high heels," Mason instructed.

"You sound mysterious."

"I am."

38

"What are we going to do?"

Mason said, "We're going to skirt the outer periphery of illegality. It is a crime to suppress evidence. It is a crime to do certain things in connection with subtracting evidence. But as far as I know, it's not a crime to add, provided it is done in the proper manner. It is only a crime to subtract."

"What, may I ask, are we going to add?" Della Street asked.

"Nothing at all," Mason said, his face a mask of innocence. "We are going to examine. We are going to take some test photographs. And, of course, as we examine and photograph, I am afraid we will leave tracks. If the officers misinterpret those tracks we can't be held responsible for their lack of acumen in judging circumstantial evidence."

"Of course not," Della Street said, smiling.

"Particularly," Mason went on, "if our efforts result in directing the attention of the officers to bits of legitimate evidence which they might overlook otherwise."

She switched out the lights, they closed the office, went to Mason's car and drove out toward the hills. Mason handed Della Street the maps, said, "I want to go up the road toward the country place where the body was discovered."

"Drake told us the police are still there," Della Street warned.

"I know," Mason said, "but it's dark and I am assuming that the activities of the police are, at the moment, centered on the place itself and not on the approaches."

"And our activities will be centered on the approaches?" she asked.

Mason nodded.

They turned off the freeway onto a paved road which after a few miles gave place to a graded country road.

Mason switched off the driving lights, turned on the parking lights and eased the car along the road, letting the motor run quietly.

Ahead they could see the bright illumination of the lodge. To the left there was a sloping hill. To the right, a cut bank.

Mason stopped the car. "Here's our place, Della."

"What do we do?"

"We get out. You follow instructions implicitly and unquestioningly. If I don't have to make explanations you won't be sure about what's in my mind."

"I think whatever is in your mind is larcenous," she said, laughing nervously.

"Not necessarily," Mason told her. "There's a narrow line of demarcation and I want to keep on the right side of that line."

He led the way across the road, which by this time had dried out enough so that footprints would not be readily visible, to the bank which was still moist. Mason said, "I'm going to lift you up on the bank. Double up your knees, then when I've pressed your back against the barbed-wire fence, hold your skirt tightly around you so it doesn't get snagged on the barbed wire and then slide down the bank. I'll catch you—I want you to leave the imprints of heels as you slide down the bank. All ready now? Here we go."

Mason picked her up, raised her to his shoulder, then pushed her back against the barbed wire. "All ready?" he asked.

"All ready," she said. "Let me go and I'll slide."

Della Street, her skirt wrapped tightly around her legs, her knees doubled up, slid down the bank and into Mason's arms.

"How's that?" she asked.

"All right," Mason said.

"Now what?" she asked.

Mason said, "I'm simply testing to see what would have happened if a girl had slid under the fence. She would have left tracks like that, wouldn't she?"

"I'm quite sure she would have—under certain circumstances," Della said.

"And in that case," Mason said, "she would have been very apt to have left a part of her skirt on the barbed wire, wouldn't she?"

"She'd be lucky if she hadn't left part of her hide on the barbed wire," Della Street rejoined.

Mason nodded, reached up and impaled the fragment of cloth he had taken from his pocket on one of the barbs. "That," he said, "should indicate what might well have

40

happened. Now we'll photograph the tracks and the fragment of cloth.''

Mason held the camera and flash gun and took two pictures.

"*You've* left some footprints here in the soft soil,'' Della Street pointed out, "and so have I.''

"I know,'' Mason said, "but I think those will be eliminated.''

"By what?''

"Police psychology,'' Mason said. "The police will first observe this piece of cloth hanging from the barbed wire. They'll jump out of the car and crowd around to inspect it. After that, they'll begin to look for tracks. They'll find our heel tracks coming down the steep bank, and only after that will they begin to wonder where the person came from who left that piece of skirt on the barbed wire and where she went to. By that time the tracks down here at the foot of the bank will all have been trampled into a hopeless mess.

"So then the police will crawl through the barbed-wire fence to look on the other side. They'll fail to find any tracks leading to this particular place but then they will find the tracks made by Arlene Ferris last night.''

"And what will they deduce from all that?'' Della Street asked.

"Heavens knows!'' Mason said. "I personally am only conducting a test. I wanted to see what sort of tracks a woman would have made in sliding down the hill, and to see whether a piece of cloth would readily impale on one of these barbs. Sometimes, you know, the barbs are dull and rusted and wouldn't be apt to catch a piece of cloth.''

"You've made your test?'' Della Street asked.

Mason nodded.

"And I take it, it would be embarrassing if a police car should come along the road and catch us here?''

Mason grinned. "Since I observe from your remark that you are hungry, I see no reason to delay getting the hell out of here and going to where we can eat.''

"Those,'' Della Street said, "are welcome words to a woman's hungry ears. Let's go.''

41

Mason backed the car down the road until he came to a wide place, turned the car, switched on his headlights and drove back to the city.

He and Della Street stopped at the photographer's studio, left films with specific instructions for development and enlargement, had dinner and then rang Paul Drake.

"Know anything new, Paul?" Mason asked.

"Very little," Drake said. "Police are checking evidence out at the place where the body was found. They're also following up the lead that Loring Lamont left the company parking place at about five-forty-five last night and that a young woman was in the car with him at that time."

"I want to talk with you about that," Mason asked.

"What are *you* going to do?" Drake asked.

"I'm driving Della home, and then I'm going to bring you some pictures."

Drake said, "Your tone sounds suspiciously smug."

"Thanks for telling me," Mason said. "I'll un-smug it."

"Moreover, I can't tell," Drake said suspiciously, "whether your smugness is because you and Della have had a very satisfactory dinner, or whether you've been up to something."

"Food," Mason said, "always leaves me in an expansive mood."

"Now," Drake said, "I *know* it was something you two have been up to."

Mason drove Della Street home, then doubled back to the photographer's office and picked up an envelope containing enlargements of Madge Elwood. He drove at once to Drake's office.

"What's cooking?" Drake asked.

Mason said, "We're stealing a card from police procedure."

"How come?"

Mason regarded Paul Drake thoughtfully. "Paul," he asked, "what's the most dangerous evidence in the world?"

"Personal identification evidence," Drake said, "the so-called infallible evidence of eyewitnesses, but it's something we can't help. Some people have accurate memories for faces and some people don't.''

Mason said, ''It goes deeper than that, Paul. It's an inherent defect in police procedure as well as in the processes of human memory.''

''How come?'' Drake asked.

Mason said, ''Suppose you should be the victim of a holdup. Police listen to your description of your assailant, they know that a certain ex-convict is in the neighborhood, they bring out mug shots of this ex-con and show them to you. They say, 'Mr. Drake, we have every reason to believe this is a picture of the man who held you up. Now don't make up your mind too hastily. Take your time. Look this picture over, study it carefully—no, no, don't shake your head—not yet. Remember that photographs sometimes look a little different from the way the individual appears—passport photographs, for instance. Sometimes you have to look several times to be sure. Now you just take your time and study that picture.'

''Then a couple of days later police ring you up and say, 'Mr. Drake, we think we have the man who held you up. We want you to come down and look at him in a police lineup.' You go down and look at the lineup. The ex-con is there. You suddenly realize he looks familiar to you. You're pretty apt to make an identification. Now, are you identifying him because you studied his picture so carefully in connection with the holdup, or are you making the identification because he's really the guy who held you up?''

''I know, I know,'' Drake said impatiently. ''It's one of those things that happen. But what the hell—human nature is human nature and you can't change it, nor can you throw out all eyewitness evidence simply because *some* guys react to the power of suggestion more than others.''

Mason grinned. ''Exactly, Paul. We're going to steal a leaf from the police book. You say that the guard who was on duty at the parking lot saw Loring Lamont drive out about a quarter to six with a good-looking young woman in the car. Police thing he can identify that woman. Now I want you to take this photograph, contact this fellow and ask him if that's

43

the woman. Ask him to take a good look at the picture, to study it carefully and see if that isn't the woman.''

"Now wait a minute," Drake said. "You're getting out on a limb there, Perry. That's tampering with a witness."

"Where's the tampering?" Mason asked.

"Well . . . you're trying to force an identification."

"I'm doing nothing of the sort," Mason said. "I'm simply asking him if he can identify a picture."

"But the way you want him to do it," Drake said, "is putting ideas in his mind."

"Isn't that the way the police do it?" Mason asked.

"Well . . . I suppose so."

"All right. Would you say the police were tampering with evidence?"

Drake accepted the snapshot reluctantly. "I'll try it," he agreed. "It may be difficult to get in touch with this fellow. The police may have him sewed up. If I go out there in a rush, trying to contact him, I'm going to arouse suspicions, and once I arouse suspicions we're . . ."

"Don't do it that way," Mason said, "Don't arouse suspicions. Don't do this in too big a hurry. On the other hand, don't let a lot of grass grow under your feet. Just take it easy, but do it at the first good opportunity."

"All right," Drake agreed. "I'll get busy on it—provided I find the guy isn't being chaperoned by the police. But I'll do it my way. I won't go out to the plant where police can check me, and I won't try to force an identification."

"Okay," Mason said, "we'll button it up for tonight, Paul. But remember to get started early in the morning."

Chapter 6

It was around eight-thirty the next morning when Perry Mason unlocked the door of his private office to find Della Street and Paul Drake studying the morning papers.

"How you coming with the photograph identification, Paul?" Mason asked.

"No dice," Paul said. "The guy works in the evening shift and sleeps late in the morning. The police sent a car out there early this morning, woke him up and took him out with them somewhere."

Mason frowned.

"I did the best I could," Drake said. "I didn't want to wake him up for fear that would push us too far out in the open. Then the police moved in and took him in tow. I have a man planted out there at the house. As soon as the guy comes back I'll be notified, and my man will show him the picture and ask questions. Incidentally, Perry, you have your name in the papers, and the police have uncovered some new evidence."

"How come?"

"A little detective work on the part of our friend, Lieutenant Tragg, who is mighty efficient when you come right down to it."

"Go ahead," Mason said, seating himself on the rounded arm of the overstuffed leather chair in which clients were made to feel at ease. "What's the pitch?"

Drake said, "When they searched the body of Loring Lamont they found, in one of his pockets, a part of a car distributor."

Mason merely nodded.

"Yesterday it turned out that Arlene Ferris, a stenographer employed at the plant, telephoned for a repair service to come out and start her car. She said she had been unable to start it the night before and thought water had leaked into the distributor. The repairman found that someone had removed a part from the distributor. It was necessary for him to get a new part and replace it.

"The part that the police found in the pocket of Loring Lamont's clothes is identical with the part that was replaced in Arlene Ferris' car, and police have reason to believe it had been removed from the distributor on her car."

"Go ahead," Mason said. "How does my name enter into it?"

"In a rather peculiar way. Yesterday afternoon Arlene Ferris served notice that she must have time off. Mr. George Albert, the office manager, stated that Miss Ferris had a most unusual attitude, that she insisted on being excused. She was away from the office something over an hour.

"Naturally, by the time the investigation reached that point, police were interested in finding out where she went and what was so urgent. By checking with the gate guard, they found that her car hadn't been moved. So their next step was to start checking with the cab company that had a stand at the corner. They had struck pay dirt by six o'clock last night. They found that Arlene Ferris had asked the driver of a cab to get her to this address as quickly as possible, that she had an appointment with a lawyer. After she had left the cab the driver noticed she had left a piece of folded paper. He picked it up and unfolded it to see if it was anything important enough to turn in to the lost-and-found department. It was just a piece of stationery of the Lamont Company with your name, address and phone number on it. He shoved it in his coat pocket. It was still there when police questioned him. He gave it to them.

"So then police got a search warrant for the apartment of Arlene Ferris."

"I see," Mason said thoughtfully.

"Police couldn't find Arlene, but they searched her apartment and found a skirt with a peculiar rip in the hem. The skirt was of a soft, woven material. Police found that a small triangular piece had been torn out of the garment. Shortly after midnight they had a hunch about the skirt. They started examining the barbed-wire fence along the road leading to the lodge where the murder had been committed. They soon found the missing piece of the garment impaled on barbed wire, with tracks showing unmistakably that some woman more interested in speed than modesty had slid under the wire, going down the bank on her back, with her feet doubled under her.

"Search of the Ferris apartment had disclosed panties bearing mud stains so police came up with the theory that Miss Ferris had been the one who slid under the fence."

"That's a crime?" Mason asked.

"Murder is a crime," Drake said dryly.

"And the police are drawing certain inferences?"

"Undoubtedly. But out of deference to the fact that Jarvis P. Lamont is a very powerful industrial tycoon, the police aren't promulgating those theories in print. They have simply stated that they are making an investigation, that they wish very much to talk with Arlene Ferris, that they wonder what caused Arlene Ferris to go to the office of Perry Mason in the middle of the afternoon and thereafter to be absent from her apartment.

"Also, police have uncovered a witness who saw a young woman park Loring Lamont's car directly in front of a fireplug. The description of that woman tallies with that of Arlene Ferris."

"Who's the witness?" Mason asked.

"A man named Jerome Henley. He lives in the apartment house where Loring Lamont has an apartment, and runs a music store—hi-fi, records, and things of that sort."

"What about the time?" Mason asked.

"Henley isn't certain of the time. His wrist watch was at the jeweler's for repair. He thought the time was ten or ten-thirty but he went to sleep right after dinner and admits he just doesn't know what time it was. He had been listening to some new records in his apartment, fell sound asleep, then wakened, went down to a lunch counter, got a cup of coffee, then went back to his apartment and to bed."

"What's the address of the place where Henley has his business?" Mason asked.

"1311 Broadside Avenue, according to the newspaper."

"All right, Paul," Mason said. "Be certain you aren't being followed. Go to see Henley. Show him the picture I gave you. Ask him if that's the young woman he saw getting out of the car."

Drake reluctantly got up out of his chair and started toward the door. "If they throw me in, you'll have to bail me out," he said, and walked out.

Mason glanced through the paper and the morning mail.

Twenty minutes later his unlisted desk phone rang and Paul Drake's excited voice came over the wire.

"It's going to work, Perry," Drake said. "At first the guy was dubious. I kept shoving the picture at him and then he began to weaken. He says she resembles the girl he saw getting out of the car and he thinks she's the one."

"Good work, Paul," Mason said.

"Here's something else," Drake said. "Lieutenant Tragg of Homicide has a stake-out on your car in the parking lot. He evidently has an idea you'll be going out and leading him to the place where your client is hiding."

"You're sure?" Mason asked.

"Of course I'm sure. It's a police car parked in front of a fireplug across the street and I'll bet it's in telephone contact with Tragg himself."

"Okay," Mason said. "I'll give that matter some thought . . . they *may* have tapped my telephone . . . be seeing you, Paul."

Mason hung up the phone, turned to Della Street.

"Della," he said, "go down to a pay telephone. Don't use the office phones. Call Madge Elwood in Santa Monica. I told her to take the day off and be available for telephone calls. Tell her to drive in at once. Give her the address of the parking lot where I keep my car.

"Now, Della, this is important. I want her to stage things so that at *exactly* ten-forty-five she drives into that parking lot. Tell her to park her car. The attendant will give her a parking ticket—so far she won't have attracted any attention."

Della Street nodded.

"I will be waiting in my automobile with the motor running and the car pointed toward the exit. As soon as she starts walking toward the exit I'll drive up alongside and open the door. At that time she is to jump in without hesitating."

"And then?" Della Street asked.

"Then," Mason said, "it depends on whether the astute Lieutenant Tragg tries to spring his trap before he finds out where we're going. I'm inclined to think that he'll give me quite a bit of rope in order to see whether I hang myself, but he may not."

"And just where *are* you going?" Della Street asked.

"Shopping," Mason said, grinning. "Now synchronize your watch with mine and tell Madge Elwood to synchronize hers with yours over the telephone. We want to do this on a split-second timing."

"Shall I tell her anything about Arlene Ferris?" Della Street asked.

"Tell her to convey a message to Arlene. Tell Arlene to sit tight for the moment, but it won't be for very long."

"Ten-forty-five on the dot," Della Street said.

"That's right. Come over here now and synchronize your watch with mine."

Della Street moved over to Perry Mason, said, "There's less than thirty seconds difference between our watches."

"Mine is right," Mason said. "I keep it right on the button. Set your watch up thirty seconds. This calls for precision timing. I want to have it click right to the second."

"But with traffic and everything," Della Street said, "she may be delayed a few seconds, even in driving around the block. It's pretty difficult to have her drive into a parking lot at exactly a certain time."

"I want it just as close to that time as she can make it," Mason said. "We have a little margin but not a great deal. Tell her that it's *exceedingly* important that she do just as I suggest."

Della Street nodded and left the office.

Chapter 7

Promptly at ten-thirty-nine Mason left his office, went down in the elevator, turned into the parking lot, nodded to the attendant, went to the stall where his car was kept, entered the car, started the motor and backed out into the lane reserved for exit, the maneuver taking him to within a few feet of the lane of incoming traffic.

At that point Mason seemed to have some trouble with his gas feed. He frowned, put his head on one side, listening to the motor, raced the throttle a few times, then let the car idle.

The time was precisely twenty seconds past ten-forty-five.

A car swung into the parking lot. The attendant stepped out of his cage, gave the driver a ticket and Madge Elwood emerged from the door shaking out her skirt.

Mason raised his hat. "Ride?" he called.

She flashed him a smile, said, "Sure," crossed around in front of the car and jumped in beside Mason.

The lawyer eased the car out of the parking lot and into the stream of traffic.

"Any trouble?" he asked.

"Not at all. I was a few seconds late. I . . . well, I was terribly nervous. I guess I misjudged the time a little."

"That's all right," Mason said. "You did very well."

"Why so particular about the time?" she asked.

Mason said, "I wanted to make my exit look natural and I would prefer not to be followed if we can avoid it."

"Why should we be followed?"

"Have you seen the papers?"

"Not the late editions."

"It's probably just as well," Mason said.

They made a right turn at the corner, then a left turn at the

50

next corner. Mason eased his way past two signals just as they were changing, then settled down to steady driving.

"Can't you circle around two or three blocks in a figure eight?" she asked. "If you think you're being followed that will enable you to find out. I read somewhere that . . ."

"Sure," Mason interrupted, "that's all right under certain circumstances but I don't want anyone to think that I'm at all suspicious. I don't want to give the impression that I'm worried about being followed. That's part of the game."

"And just what is the game?"

Mason smiled and said, "Act perfectly natural. That's all you need to do."

Mason drove conservatively, turned into Broadside Avenue, found a parking lot in the 1200 block and said to Madge Elwood, "We walk a block. How's Arlene getting along?"

"All right," she said. "She had trouble sleeping but I gave her some sleeping pills I had and they worked all right."

"And this morning?"

"She's feeling better. She is, of course, bursting with curiosity, but I told her to leave everything to you. She's dying to know what you wanted with me but I couldn't help her very much there because I didn't know myself."

"That's right," Mason said, offering no further explanation.

Abruptly the lawyer said, "Are you interested in music? In the new records?"

"I'm crazy about the new stereophonic gadgets," she said.

"Well, let's go in and look around," Mason told her, and taking her elbow in his hand, piloted her through the door of a store which featured hi-fi equipment and records in the window.

A salesman came forward and Mason said, "I'd like to discuss a deal for a complete hi-fi installation."

"Yes, indeed," the salesman bowed.

"You are the manager here?"

"I'm the head salesman."

"There is, I believe, a Mr. Henley here."

"He owns the place."

"Is he available?"

"That's the man there, in the office."

"The one behind the glass partition?"

"That's right."

"I think I'd like to talk with him," Mason said, "about the installation. Would you mind?"

"I know he'll be glad to come over," the salesman said.

"Well, we can walk over there," Mason said. "I don't want to bother him and I don't want to do anything that would interfere with any commission or bonus arrangement you might have. Would you mind asking him a question for me?"

"Certainly not."

"Ask him if he knows Jim Billings," Mason said. "I think Mr. Billings got his equipment here."

"Very well," the salesman said, and walked toward the glass-enclosed office.

Mason followed him, to stand just outside the glassed-in office.

The salesman approached Henley, who listened, looked up, frowned, then following the nod of the salesman's head, looked toward Mason and Madge Elwood.

Henley hesitated a moment, then arose from his chair and walked to the door of the office.

"Good morning," he said. "There was some question about a Mr. Billings? I don't believe I recall the name but I can assure you that we're prepared to give you the best service, the best prices and . . ."

"Just a minute," a dry voice cut in from behind Mason. "We'll take charge here now."

Mason turned. "Why, Lieutenant Tragg! What are *you* doing here?"

"I just happened to be in the neighborhood," Lt. Tragg said. "You see, we talked with Jerome Henley earlier in the day—in fact, quite early this morning. Mr. Henley and I are by way of being old friends."

Tragg turned to Henley and said, "Do you know this man, Henley?"

The manager shook his head.

"All right," Tragg said. "For your information, this is Mr. Perry Mason, the famous attorney who specializes in trial work and primarily in defending persons accused of murder. I don't know who this young woman is. That doesn't make any difference. I want you to look at her carefully before you answer my next question.

"I don't like to impugn Mr. Mason's motives but I am very much afraid the astute lawyer is trying one of his tricks by which he confuses a witness whom he expects to cross-examine. This is something he's done before. If a witness is going to identify someone . . . if there is any possibility *you*, for instance, might be called on to identify this young woman as the person you saw getting out of Loring Lamont's car when it was parked in front of the fireplug a couple of nights ago, Mr. Mason could bring her into your store where you'd see her casually.

"Then later on, when you get on the witness stand and identify her as the woman who got out of Lamont's car, Mr. Mason could smile fiendishly at you and say on cross-examination, 'Aren't you mistaken? Isn't *this* the young woman who was in your store with me when I was asking you about hi-fi equipment?''

"Now, Henley, I don't want you to get trapped. I don't want you to speak up until you're certain. Have you ever seen this young woman before? Is this the woman who got out of Loring Lamont's car?"

Mason said, "And don't let *him* confuse you, Henley. This is no way to make an identification. If this young woman is . . ."

"She is!" Henley interrupted. "*That's* the woman I saw get out of the car. She was dressed a little differently but that's the woman."

"Now be sure. Be absolutely sure," Lt. Tragg said.

"I'm sure that's the woman."

Tragg turned to Mason with a smile. "Won't you introduce me, Mason?" he said. "Or perhaps there's no need for you to do it. Miss Arlene Ferris, I am Lieutenant Tragg of Homicide and I'd like to ask you a few questions about where you were on the night Loring Lamont was murdered."

Madge Elwood stepped back with an exclamation of dismay so well done that even Mason was fooled. Her face actually seemed to go white to the lips.

"Come, come, now," Tragg said. "If you're innocent there's nothing to be afraid of, and . . ."

Mason interrupted. "I'm afraid you have made a slight mistake, Lieutenant. Miss Elwood, permit me to present Lieutenant Tragg. Lieutenant Tragg, this is Madge Elwood, a secretary from Santa Monica. She also happens to be interested in hi-fi equipment so I brought her in here to listen to some of the latest equipment."

Tragg's voice suddenly was edged with sharp authority. "You're sure?" he asked Henley.

"I'm absolutely certain, Lieutenant. That's the woman."

"I thought it would be," Tragg said. "We'll unscramble the names later. That's Mason for you! You can see the trap he was setting for you. He'd have asked you a question or two, then walked out. You are busy. There is no reason for you to remember two customers who make a casual inquiry.

"Later on, when you identified this girl, Mason would have convinced the jury your subconscious had played a trick on you, that you remembered her as the girl who had been in here with him."

"I see," Henley said. He leaned slightly forward, looking at Madge Elwood. His forehead creased with a frown.

Tragg said harshly, "You've raised hell if this isn't the girl."

"Tut-tut, such language," Mason said reproachfully.

"It's the girl," Henley said at length.

Tragg turned to Perry Mason. "We can dispense with your company, Counselor. Miss Elwood and I are going to take a little ride."

"You've got a warrant?" Mason asked.

"I don't need one," Tragg said.

"You need one in order to take her into custody and dispense with my company," Mason said. "If you're going to take a ride I'm going with you. You can't take Miss Elwood away from me simply on your say-so."

"She has just been identified as . . ."

"I have good ears," Mason said. "I heard the identifica-

54

tion. I heard how positive it was. Just remember that when we get to court.''

''I don't know what kind of a razzle-dazzle you're trying at the moment,'' Tragg said, ''but I'm going to find out. Come on, Miss Elwood, you're coming with me.''

''And I'm coming along,'' Mason said.

Tragg hesitated a moment, then yielded the point. ''Very well,'' he said, ''but you're not going to interfere in any way. You're going to keep quiet. I'm going to do the talking. If you try to confuse the witness, I'm going to dust off a few sections of the Penal Code which you may have forgotten.''

Mason's smile was urbane. ''Come, come, Lieutenant,'' he said, ''I never *forget* any of the sections of the Penal Code. I can't afford to.''

Tragg said to Madge Elwood, ''We're going in a police car. Come on.''

He led the way outside to where the police car with a driver was waiting at the curb.

Tragg held the rear door open for Madge Elwood and the lawyer.

Mason, catching her eye, made a gesture for silence.

They entered the car. Tragg said something in a low voice to the driver, and the car eased out into traffic, then purred into swift speed.

The car veered off into a residential district of rather modest houses. Tragg and the driver held a low-voiced conversation. Tragg indicated a street, the driver turned to the left and stopped in front of a small bungalow.

Tragg said, ''You folks wait here.''

He went to the house, rang the bell and after the door was opened, went inside. He was in for about five minutes, then came out accompanied by a man who walked with him to the automobile.

Tragg stood with his back to the car, the man facing him. They said nothing for a few moments, then Tragg said, ''We'll try not to detain you. Look at the other side.''

They walked around the automobile. The man apparently was inspecting the police car.

After a moment Tragg led the way back into the house.

55

He was in there for another five minutes, then came out and said to the driver, "All right. Take them back to the music store."

"May I ask what this is all about?" Mason asked.

"Sure you can ask," Tragg said.

"Will you tell me?"

"I'll let you guess."

Mason said, "I suppose this car was in an accident somewhere and you wanted the man to identify it."

Tragg grinned. "Could be."

"Or perhaps the city is thinking of selling police cars as surplus and this man wants to buy," Mason went on.

"Could be," Tragg said in a tone of voice which didn't invite further speculation or conversation.

They rode in silence back to the music store. "All right," Tragg said, "this is where we picked you up, this is where we let you out."

"Thanks," Mason told him. "Any time we can be of service, just let us know—how did it happen you located me in that music store, Lieutenant?"

"I just happened to be in the neighborhood," Tragg said, "and saw you in there, so I thought I'd keep you from sabotaging the People's case by putting Henley in a spot where he'd be vulnerable on cross-examination."

"He's vulnerable now," Mason said.

"I'm not arguing," Tragg said. "They pay me to investigate cases, not to argue with lawyers. Come on, Frank, let's go."

The car moved away from the curb.

"Mr. Mason," Madge Elwood said in a panic, "you can't let them do that to me! This man in the music store, he has no right to say that he saw me getting out of a car. I was in Santa Monica and . . ."

"Take it easy," Mason said, "take it easy. I think Lieutenant Tragg didn't seem too happy as he drove off. Let's see if we can find out the cause of his unhappiness."

"What are you going to do?" she asked.

"Take a ride," Mason said. "Come on, let's go."

He went to the parking lot, got out his car and started driving.

"But this is the same way that the police officers went," she said at length.

"I know," Mason said.

"You're going back to that same house?"

Mason nodded.

"Why?"

"Just to check up," Mason said.

She started to protest, then lapsed into silence. Mason drove the car back to the bungalow, parked it, went up to the house and rang the bell.

The same man who had walked out to look at the car answered the door, started to say something, then said, "You're the man who was out here with the police a short time ago?"

"That's right," Mason told him.

"I told the Lieutenant all I know," the man said. "I can't be sure. It looks like the girl, but I can't be sure it's the same one. A man was out here with a picture. He asked me if I could identify the picture. I told him I couldn't. I think the girl with the police was the one whose picture I saw.

"I only had a quick glimpse as Loring Lamont drove his car out of the parking lot. There was a girl with him. I'm not certain this is the one."

"Thank you very much," Mason said. "I'm sorry I bothered you."

"Not at all. The police woke me up early this morning. I can't go back to sleep. I'd like to help, but I'm not going to say I'm sure if I'm not sure, and that's that."

"I know exactly how you feel," Mason told him, "and I respect your feelings. What's your name again?"

"Tom Grimes."

"Thanks a lot," Mason said, shaking hands. "I'll try not to bother you again."

He walked back to the car.

"Now, let's not misunderstand each other," he said to Madge Elwood. "You're willing to do anything you can to help Arlene?"

57

"That's right."

"I'm going to mix you up in this thing," Mason said.

"How deep?" she asked apprehensively.

"Not so deep that you can't get out," Mason told her. "They're going to drop you like a hot potato but I want to be sure they get their fingers pretty badly burned before they do it. All right with you?"

"Anything you say is all right with me, Mr. Mason. The main thing I want to do is to help Arlene. I'll . . . I'll do anything—absolutely anything to help her."

"All right," Mason said. "I'll take you back to the parking lot. Get your car and drive to your apartment. Newspaper reporters will be there shortly after you arrive. Go home now and fix yourself up for the photographers. I want you to take good pictures."

"Cheesecake?" she asked.

"Within moderate limits," Mason said. "Don't let them overdo it."

Chapter 8

Mason returned to his office to find Paul Drake waiting for him.

"The police have picked up Arlene Ferris," Drake said.

"Where did they find her?" Mason asked.

"Down at Santa Monica, in the apartment of a friend."

"How did they get the lead?" Mason asked. "What started them down there searching for her?"

"I don't know. They probably started checking on all of her friends."

Mason said to Della Street, "Get me Hamilton Burger on the phone. I'd like to talk with him personally, but if I can't do that I'll talk with his chief deputy."

"Going right to the top, eh?" Drake asked.

"Going right to the top," Mason said.

He watched while Della Street relayed the call through the switchboard in the outer office, then, after a moment when she nodded and said, "The district attorney is coming on the phone," Mason took the phone.

"Hello, Burger," Mason said.

Hamilton Burger's voice was cautious. "Hello, Mr. Mason, what can I do for you?"

"The police are picking up one of my clients, an Arlene Ferris."

"Yes," Hamilton Burger said. "They want to question her in connection with the murder of Loring Lamont."

"All right," Mason said. "She's my client. If you question her I want to be there."

"I have no intention of questioning her. Someone in my office may be present, but the police will probably conduct the interrogation."

"That's just dandy," Mason said. "Now, as soon as she's brought in I want to have it understood that I talk with her."

Burger said, "Well, don't complain to me about it, Mason. Take it up with the police. You know how they work as well as I do. They've probably questioned her at some length, and by the time they bring her in and book her the questioning will have been completed."

Mason said, "A word from your office to the police might save us both a lot of trouble. I want to have the privilege of visiting her as her attorney as soon as she is brought into detention, whether she's booked, or not."

"Well, why not take it up with the police?"

"I'm taking it up with you," Mason said. "With your assistance, I can do it the easy way. Without your assistance I'll have to do it the hard way."

"What's the hard way?" Burger asked.

"Habeas corpus," Mason said. "That will put us both to a bit of trouble."

Hamilton Burger thought for a moment, then said, "I'm quite certain you won't have any trouble visiting her as soon as she's brought in—provided, of course, you are her attorney."

"I'm her attorney."

"All right. Let me ask you a couple of questions. I happen to know something about this case personally. When she heard Loring Lamont had been murdered why didn't she come to the police and say that she had been out with Lamont at the scene of the murder the night that it occurred—that is, of course, assuming that she's innocent?"

"Well," Mason said, "that brings up a nice question. When did she learn that he had been murdered?"

"You're asking me questions in answer to my questions," Burger said.

"I don't know any other way to handle the situation."

Burger said, "I'll tell you this much frankly, Mason. If she's innocent we don't want to drag her through a lot of publicity. If she's guilty, naturally we want to prosecute her—unless, of course, you'd like to consider entering a guilty

60

plea. And if it was self-defense, she'd better come out and say so right now.''

Mason said, ''I'll discuss the matter with my client.''

''You're already discussed it with her probably half a dozen times,'' Burger said.

''You might be surprised,'' Mason told him.

''All right, all right,'' Burger said testily. ''You won't need to file a habeas corpus, you get to talk with her as soon as she's brought in. But I don't think the police are going to bring her in until after they've asked her a lot of questions.''

''Quite all right with me,'' Mason said. ''I take it you're personally familiar with the details of the case?''

''I'm getting familiar with them. The Lamont family is rather prominent. This is hardly a run-of-the-mill murder case.''

''Okay,'' Mason told him. ''I'll rely on your promise to fix things so I can see my client as soon as she's brought in. Thanks a lot.''

Mason hung up, turned to Paul Drake. ''Know anything else, Paul?''

''This much,'' Drake said. ''Loring Lamont went out to that lodge. He had a young woman with him. They cooked ham and eggs and a plate of hot biscuits, and then sat down and ate. Lamont was killed within a matter of minutes after the meal.''

''Both of them ate?'' Mason asked.

''Both of them ate.''

Mason frowned thoughtfully.

''What have you found out about that place out there, Paul?''

''Well, it's maintained by the company as a place of entertainment.''

''Any caretaker or anybody in charge?''

''Yes. There's a woman who lives about five miles down the road, who keeps the place clean.''

''What's her name?''

''Sadie Richmond, a widow.''

''What else?''

''The place is completely surrounded by a woven-mesh,

heavy-wire fence, ten feet high, with strings of barbed wire across the top. You either get in through the gate or you don't get in at all. The gate is kept locked. They're very careful to keep it locked at all times because there's a swimming pool there and they don't want to be responsible for anybody who might blunder into the swimming pool and get drowned.''

"There's no way a person could drive in except along that road through the gate?''

"That's right.''

"No back gate, no back entrance to the property?''

"Nothing.''

"What about Sadie Richmond?''

"She goes in every day, usually between ten o'clock and noon. She straightens the place up. Sometimes people will be out there and leave dirty glasses, dirty dishes and generally mess the place up. She keeps it clean.

"There are a couple of bedrooms in the place and sometimes executives of the company or their friends will sleep out there. Sadie keeps the beds changed with fresh linen. A man comes in, in the afternoons, and keeps the yard in condition. A pool company services the swimming pool, and their representative has a key to the gate. It's a heated swimming pool with a thermostat and it's kept at an even temperature all year round.''

Mason glanced at his watch. "How long ago did the police pick up Arlene Ferris, Paul?''

"I can't tell for certain, but it must have been nearly an hour.''

Mason frowned. "They evidently got there soon after Madge Elwood left the apartment. Come on, Paul, we're going to take a run out and look the property over—the scene of the crime.''

"We can't get in,'' Drake said.

"What'll you bet?'' Mason asked.

"Now, wait a minute, Perry, let's not try anything that's going to make trouble.''

"The police are finished out there?''

"The police have finished, the newspaper reporters have

been admitted and given an opportunity to take photographs, and now the place is closed up tight as a drum.''

"That suits me fine," Mason said. "Let's go hunt up Sadie Richmond. You have her address?"

Drake nodded.

"Okay," Mason said. "Let's go."

"Want me?" Della Street asked.

Mason hesitated a moment, then nodded his head. "Come on," he said, "a woman's eye may detect certain things that would escape a man."

"What are you looking for?" Paul Drake asked.

"If I knew," Mason told him, "I wouldn't have to go out. Come on, let's go."

The three of them went down to the parking lot, got in Mason's car, drove out along the freeway, then turned off at the point Drake designated. After a short distance they turned from the pavement to a dirt road.

"Sadie Richmond lives along in here," Drake said.

Mason slowed the car.

"This is the place. Turn in here," Drake said.

Mason turned in to a neat little bungalow, stopped the car, said, "Now let's see if we get this straight, Paul. You can't get in without a key?"

"That's right."

"But there are several keys—the executives of the company have them, Sadie Richmond has one, the swimming-pool people have one, the man who takes care of the place has one."

"That's right."

"What's his name?"

"Otto Keswick."

"Where does he live?"

"About half a mile up the road here."

"All right," Mason said. "Let's go see Sadie Richmond."

They left the car, walked up the steps of the bungalow and Mason rang the bell.

The woman who came to the door was in her early thirties, a rather large woman, but a woman who carried no extra weight and moved with lithe grace. She had a well-modeled figure.

Mason introduced himself.

"I'm interested in the Loring Lamont case," he said.

"Who isn't?" Sadie Richmond asked, with a ghost of a smile.

"Have you been in the place this morning to clean up?"

"The police don't want it cleaned up, not for a while."

"Have you been out there this morning?"

"No, I haven't been out there yet. Police asked me to wait until they telephoned that it was all right to go in. They removed quite a few articles, I understand."

"You haven't been notified yet?"

"Yes, they notified me about half an hour ago and said it was all right, that they were finished with the place."

"So you're going in to clean up?"

"That's right."

"How would you like some help?" Mason asked.

She smiled and shook her head.

Mason opened his wallet, took out a twenty-dollar bill.

Sadie Richmond looked at the bill. Her face became wooden. She said nothing.

Mason took out a second twenty-dollar bill, then another and another. He smoothed them out, then folded them and folded them once more, making them into a compact packet.

"We wouldn't get in the way at all," he promised.

Sadie Richmond smiled and shook her head.

Mason said, "Look here, a young woman is accused of that murder. I'm representing her. The police are finished with the place. There's no more evidence out there. I'd like to get familiar with the place so I can represent this young woman intelligently.

"I don't know how much you know about Loring Lamont's personal life, but this young woman was lured out there and . . . and now she's charged with murder. I'm representing her. I want to see the place. I can get a court order letting me in, but that's going to take time. My time is worth money."

He handed Sadie Richmond the eighty dollars. She hesitated a moment, then closed her hand over the money. "I don't know about what happened the night of the murder," she said dryly, "but I've seen things sometimes when I was cleaning up that . . . well . . ."

"Yes?" Mason asked, as she hesitated.

"I'm not saying anything," she said.

"Nothing?" Mason asked.

"Nothing. But you can come along. I guess there's no law against that, is there?"

Mason said, "I told you I thought I could get a court order to let me in if I had to."

"You wouldn't need to tell anyone that I let you in."

"I'm the soul of discretion," Mason said.

"All right," Sadie Richmond said. "I'll go in my car, you go in yours. I'll go first and unlock the gate. I guess I've got a lot of work to do out there this morning."

"Dirty dishes?" Mason asked.

"The police took the dishes."

"All of them?"

"All of the dirty ones."

"Well," Mason told her, "that'll simplify the job. All right, we'll get in our car and drive out to the road. You go right ahead and we'll follow."

Sadie Richmond, driving a rather beaten-up, old-model car, came out of the driveway, turned into the dirt road and sent her car into speed. The roadway had now dried out sufficiently so that there was a faint trace of dust behind the wheels, and Mason, following closely, had fine particles of dirt thrown up against his car by the speeding rear wheels.

Drake said dryly, "I guess they don't pay her portal-to-portal. She believes in getting on the job once she starts . . . my gosh, Perry, that woman drives like the devil."

Mason, concentrating on his driving to keep reasonably close to the car ahead, grinned and said nothing.

At length the woman braked her car to a stop, jumped out and unlocked the big padlock, left the chain dangling on the gate, threw the gate open and drove through.

Mason followed, stopped his car behind hers. She jumped out, closed the gate and locked it.

"We're supposed to keep it locked—always," she said.

"You have good brakes on that car," Drake observed.

She looked at him blankly.

"Otherwise you'd have wound up in the swimming pool."

There was no expression on her face. "We're not allowed to use the swimming pool," she said. She got in her car and swung around the driveway to stop at the back of the house.

"That's for you and your wisecracks," Della Street said, laughing.

"Now there's a woman for you," Drake said. "She looks innocent enough on the surface, but—well, I'd hate to sit in a poker game with her."

"She might take the pot with a pair of deuces," Mason said, as he emerged from the car and walked around to open the door for Della Street.

Della slid to the ground with a quick flash of shapely legs. "Want me to bring a book?" she asked.

"I don't think so," Mason said, "Just a small notebook."

"I have one in my purse. There are some big notebooks in the glove compartment."

"The small one will be all right," Mason said.

They followed Sadie Richmond into the house.

"Well, here it is," she said.

Mason looked around at the sumptuous rustic furnishings, the Navaho rugs, the kitchen with its electric stove, garbage disposal, dishwashing machine, the array of copper-bottomed pots and pans hanging above the stove.

"Fixed up for cooking," he observed.

"Occasionally they have barbecues out here. Mr. J. P. Lamont is a very fine cook. When they have barbecues they have me out here to serve and wash the dishes."

"A walk-in icebox?" Mason asked.

"No, just that one refrigerator there. They bring out steaks when they're having a barbecue. They don't keep much here except some ham and a lot of eggs. Occasionally they have a few pounds of bacon. They want it so if they get stuck out here on some kind of a conference they can fix themselves up a snack. But they don't go in for cooking out here except when they have the barbecues. Then they bring out all the food.''

"Mr. Lamont is a good cook?'' Mason asked.

She sighed and said, ''Like all men cooks, he can dirty more damn dishes than anybody you ever saw.''

Della Street laughed.

Mason looked at the chalked outline on the floor and the sinister reddish tinge. "I take it this is where the body was.''

"I guess that's right,'' she said. ''They told me to clean it up. I don't know whether old J. P. intends to give me a bonus or not, but my job certainly isn't supposed to include cleaning up the blood from dead bodies.''

"I take it you've worked on parties given by Loring Lamont,'' Mason said.

"*His* parties were just for two,'' she said, and turned abruptly away.

Mason nodded to Paul Drake. They started looking through the house, and when Sadie Richmond made no objection, began opening and closing drawers, looking in closets.

"No clothes out here?'' Mason asked.

"No. J. P. Lamont keeps some coveralls that he uses when he's putting on a barbecue, and there are a couple of cook aprons up there on the shelf, but they don't keep any clothes out here except playclothes—shorts, swimsuits, things like that. Down by the pool they have a few dressing rooms where they keep a supply of swimsuits for guests.''

Mason moved over to a writing desk.

"Why the writing desk?'' he asked.

"I don't know,'' she said. ''It's always been here.''

"Anybody ever use it?''

"I use it.''

"What for?''

"I keep my bills in there, things that I pay out for running the house—laundry bills and things of that sort.''

Mason opened the desk, the door of which swung down to make a writing shelf, and looked casually through the pigeonholes.

"Hello,'' he said. ''What's this?''

Mrs. Richmond looked over Mason's shoulder.

"A checkbook," she said.

"Yours?"

"Heavens, no. I don't use a checkbook."

Mason said, "There are only four or five checks used out of it. It's on the California Second National."

Mason looked at the check stubs. "One a week ago to an automobile agency for seventy-eight dollars and fifty cents. One to the Endicott Arms Holding Corporation for six hundred and twenty-five dollars. One for five hundred to Orval Kingman. That was dated . . . that was dated on the day of the murder. Here's another one for five hundred—the last one in the book. The stub says simply 'O.K.' "

Mason looked at the figures on the side of the stub. "There's a balance of twenty-five hundred seventeen dollars and thirty cents."

"Where was it?" Mrs. Richmond asked.

"In this pigeonhole, with all these papers," Mason said, spreading out some receipted bills and some bills which hadn't been receipted: one from the company which serviced the pool marked "O.K.," another from the laundry marked "O.K."

"What are these?"

"Bills that are to be picked up and paid," she said. "Whenever anyone comes out here they pick up the bills."

"And the O.K.?" Mason asked.

"That's what I put on them when they're to be paid."

"What about this check stub?" Mason asked. "Did you put the O.K. on there?"

She shook her head and said, "I wouldn't okay check stubs. Why would I?"

"That," Mason said, "is a fair question."

"What do you mean by that?"

"I was just wondering why you would okay it."

"Well, then, why did you ask?"

"Simply because you had marked 'O.K.' on the bills and I wanted to see if you had put the 'O.K.' on this."

"Well, I told you," she said. And then suddenly, with her manner changing, said, "You wanted to get in here in order

68

to see the premises. You've seen them—nothing was said about you going around opening drawers and desks and looking at papers."

"We'd like to look around," Mason said, "just to familiarize ourselves with . . ."

"Well, you've done it now. You're acquainted with what the place looks like."

Mason said suavely, "As I understand it, Loring Lamont was stabbed with a butcher knife. I wonder if you could tell us where that knife came from, if there's one short here in the kitchen, or . . ."

"I couldn't tell you a thing," she said. "You wanted to get in and you've got in. The more I think of it, the more I think it might be worth my job if anyone knew about this. Come on, you're going out."

She marched determinedly toward the door.

As she had her back turned, Mason slipped the checkbook into his inside coat pocket. "All right," he said, "if you feel it might jeopardize your job, we certainly don't want to do that."

"I'll let you out the gate," she said, "and lock the gate behind you when you go out. I don't think Mr. Lamont would like the idea of me letting you in here . . . in fact, I know he wouldn't."

She marched out through the door, left her car where it was, walked down to the gate, took out a key, unlocked the big padlock, swung the gate back and stood waiting.

"Well," Mason said, as they got in the car, "there seems to have been an abrupt change in her manner."

"The soul of cordiality, isn't she," Drake said.

"You can't blame her," Della Street said. "Personally, I think you swept her off her feet with that eighty dollars and she decided to take a chance. But the more she thinks of it, the more she realizes she can get into trouble, and . . ."

Mason started the car. "It was that checkbook that changed her manner," he said.

"Sure," Della Street told him. "She suddenly realized that you were uncovering evidence and that you might use

69

it, and then people would want to know how you happened to know about it."

"Where's my camera?" Mason asked.

"The little 35 mm. is in the glove compartment."

"We've got an adjustment on there for closeups?"

"There's one in the case," Della Street said. "Do you want it?"

"Maybe we'd better have it," Mason said.

Della Street opened the glove compartment, took out the camera. Mason held the checkbook up in the sun. "Put on the closeup attachment, Della. We can take a picture at a hundredth of a second, and . . . just be sure it's in focus."

Della Street adjusted the camera.

"Come on, come on, hurry up," Sadie Richmond called from the gate. "I can't stay here all day."

Mason held the checkbook in the sunlight. Della Street, holding the camera only a few inches from the checkbook, snapped one picture after another as Mason turned the check stubs.

"Got it?" Mason asked.

"Got it," Della Street said.

Abruptly Sadie Richmond left her position at the gate and came striding toward them. "Now look," she said, "I told you to get out. I don't want anyone to catch you here. You've been here long enough."

Mason said, "We appreciate your position, Mrs. Richmond. Here, incidentally, is the checkbook, which I held onto because I wanted to study it. You'd better put it back in the desk where it was."

"You didn't have any right to take that."

"We didn't take it," Mason said. "Now, may I suggest, Mrs. Richmond, that you call this checkbook to the attention of the police. I think it's evidence."

"Evidence of what?"

"I don't know."

"Neither do I," Sadie Richmond said, literally snatching the checkbook out of Mason's hand. "Now, will you please get going."

70

Mason raised his hat. "Thank you very much," he said.

"Don't mention it," she snapped.

The lawyer started the car and they drove out. Behind him, Sadie Richmond swung the gate shut and clicked the padlock into place.

"Now, Paul," Mason said, "it's up to you to find out whether that checkbook was the property of Loring Lamont and who Orval Kingman is."

"You think it's his checkbook?" Drake asked. "The way she acted, it looked as though she might have something to do with it. It might be that she's got an account she doesn't want anyone to know about."

"It could be," Mason said, "but whoever wrote that last check wrote it after the check to Orval Kingman, dated the day of the murder, was written. The check may well have been payable to cash and—well, it's a strange thing that Sadie Richmond puts 'O.K.' on the bills that are to be paid and that someone put 'O.K.' on the stub of a check made for five hundred dollars. If that checkbook should turn out to be Loring Lamont's checkbook it's a valuable piece of evidence."

"How come?" Drake asked. "Perhaps he keeps it there in the desk and . . ."

"He couldn't, Paul—that is, I don't think he did. It was taken from his pocket. The checks were checks that had been made over a period of four or five days and included a check for a garage bill and apparently a check for the rent on his apartment. Now, he wouldn't have kept his checkbook in the desk out there in that rustic retreat and driven out there in order to have picked up the checkbook, written the check to the car agency that serviced his car, then written a check for his apartment rental."

"Suppose it's somebody else's checkbook."

"Then," Mason said, "it's the checkbook of someone who lives in the Endicott Arms Apartments."

"Well, anyhow," Della Street said, "we've got a clue."

"To what?" Drake asked.

"That," Mason said, "is the thing which interests me.

71

You get to work on that, Paul. I'm going to talk with my client and see if *she* can give us any information that will be of any help.''

Chapter 9

Mason sat in the conference room reserved for attorneys and regarded Arlene Ferris thoughtfully. "Now you've told me everything?" he asked.

"Every single blessed thing," she said.

Mason said, "They're filing charges against you. They seem to be very confident. I'm satisfied they have some hidden evidence that I don't know anything about."

"Well, I don't know what it could be. I didn't kill him. I know that." And then, after a moment, she said savagely, "Sometimes I wish I had. If I'd got hold of that knife I . . ."

"Tut-tut," Mason interrupted. "None of that. Now, you did tell your story to the police?"

"I did. I probably shouldn't have, but this Lieutenant Tragg of Homicide was no nice and fatherly, and he seemed—well, it seemed as though he really didn't *want* to take me into custody. He wanted me to explain, if I could."

"Yes, I know," Mason said. "That's part of the police technique. And you told him?"

"I told him."

"Everything?"

"Everything."

Mason frowned thoughtfully. "Now look," he said, "we'll be in court within a few days on a preliminary hearing. The purpose of that hearing is to find out if there's sufficient cause to hold you on a criminal charge. But we have the right to ask questions and we have the right to call witnesses. It usually doesn't do any good to call witnesses, but it does give us an opportunity to size up the prosecution's case.

"There are certain things that we know happened. Loring

Lamont must have walked back to the cabin, and he must have eaten the ham and eggs almost immediately."

"Why do you say almost immediately?"

"Because," Mason said, "cold ham and eggs wouldn't be very palatable. Now, you're certain there were two plates of ham and eggs?"

"Yes. I had just placed the eggs on the plates."

"Then someone was there to eat that other plate of ham and eggs and some of the biscuits," Mason said. "Now, that someone must have been there within a matter of minutes of the time you left—how many cars did you meet on the road?"

"Not a one, not until after I had left the graveled road and got to the highway."

"Think carefully," Mason said. "Are you sure? There must have been *some* car that came along and . . ."

She shook her head vehemently. "No, I know there wasn't any other car."

Mason frowned thoughtfully. After a moment, he said, "Now, as you tell the story, there was a remarkable change in his tactics after he got that last telephone call. He was playing it for a long, cozy evening prior to that time, then suddenly he got rough."

"I'll say he did!"

"Something in that conversation changed his entire plan of operation," Mason said. "He knew he had to speed up his approach. Someone was coming. Was there any clue as to who it was?"

She shook her head. "I didn't pay too much attention to the conversation. He wasn't doing much talking—at least until after he left the one telephone and went back to the extension line."

"He was doing *some* talking, all right," Mason said. "The fact that he went to the extension line indicates that he was going to say something that he didn't want you to hear. What did he say when he picked up the telephone? Wasn't there anything that would give you a clue as to the person he was talking with?"

She shook her head.

"No names?"

"I'm quite sure he didn't mention any names."

"You don't know whether it was a man or a woman from the nature of the conversation, from what he said?"

"No, I don't . . . he seemed to be agreeing with this person, though. It wasn't anyone he was arguing with."

"What makes you say that?"

"Well, he kept saying, 'All right, all right.' "

"Was that what he said, 'All right'?"

"Yes, and I remember he kept saying, 'Okay.' He said something about . . ."

Mason came bolt upright. "Wait a minute!" he snapped. "Try and remember just what he said about okay."

"Well, he said, 'Hello', and then he said, 'Hi.' You know, the way you would talk to someone you knew intimately, and then he said something about okay, and I think he said, 'All right,' or something, I just can't remember, Mr. Mason, but I do remember he said, 'Okay,' and I think at one time he said, 'All right, okay.' I remember it sounded just a little strange for him to agree twice."

"Then okay could have been his nickname for the person he was talking with," Mason said excitedly. "Someone whose initials were O.K."

"Yes, that could have been the case, all right. That would have accounted for it."

"All right," Mason said. "Don't say anything about this to anyone. Keep a stiff upper lip and we'll do the best we can. You've done your talking. Don't talk any more and don't tell anyone about this telephone conversation, about this O.K. Just keep quiet from now on."

Mason got to his feet.

"I wish I could have remembered a little more, Mr. Mason. I . . . well, I have always been trained *not* to listen in on other people's conversations—you know how it is. I just . . . well, I probably wouldn't have noticed it at all if it hadn't been for the fact that the food was hot and I . . . I was proud of those biscuits and I wanted him to eat them while they were hot. Biscuits can get soggy rather quickly, and . . ."

"I know," Mason said. "Don't worry about it. I'll do the worrying from now on. I probably won't see you again until after you're brought into court. Just sit tight and keep a stiff upper lip.''

Mason left the visiting room and hurried to his office.

"Anything new?" Della Street asked.

"Lots," Mason said. "I want to find out about Orval Kingman. Have we heard anything from Paul?"

"Not yet. He said . . . here he is now," she said, as Drake's code knock sounded on the locked exit door of Mason's office.

"All right, Paul," Mason said, as Della opened the door, "I've got something for you. This check that was made to 'O.K.' may be damned important. O.K. may not mean what we think it means. It may be the initials of the person to whom the check was payable. Now, there's one check to Orval Kingman and . . ."

"I've got the dope on Orval Kingman," Drake said. "He's a bookie."

Mason raised his eyebrows.

"A high-class bookie," Drake said, "and I wouldn't be too surprised if Loring Lamont didn't give him quite a bit of business."

"Now that," Mason said thoughtfully, "would account for a lot of things."

"Wait a minute," Della Street said, opening her notebook. "We've got one more O.K."

"What do you mean?" Mason asked.

"Otto Keswick, the gardener who takes care of the yard."

Mason became suddenly thoughtful. "Darned if we haven't," he said. "What do you know about Otto Keswick, Drake? Have you found anything on him?"

"I have a report on him," Drake said. "I haven't met him. I can tell you one thing about him—he's a parolee."

"The devil!" Mason said. "What was he in for?"

"Blackmail," Drake said.

Mason turned to Della Street. "Get those films of the checkbook developed right away, and . . ."

"They're already being developed," she said. "I've left word for enlargements and I have an appointment with a

76

handwriting expert who will perhaps be able to tell whether the O.K. is in the handwriting of Loring Lamont.''

''What are the chances?'' Mason asked.

''Pretty good,'' she said, ''if we have any other O.K. written by Loring Lamont to use as an exemplar. Otherwise, the chances aren't quite so good. He can probably tell whether the other writing on the check stubs was written by Loring Lamont, but just two letters that way are going to be pretty difficult unless we have some other places where Loring Lamont has written O.K.''

Mason nodded, said, ''And we can probably produce some bills with an O.K. written by Sadie Richmond and see if she wrote that O.K. on the check stub. However, if it's Loring Lamont's checkbook, the chances are a hundred to one it's Loring Lamont's writing.''

Mason was thoughtful for a moment, then said, ''Paul, get in touch with the tellers at the bank on which that check was drawn. I want to find out who presents that five-hundred-dollar check to be cashed.''

''They won't pay it?''

''Not unless it was paid before banking hours on the night Loring Lamont was killed. They won't cash any checks after a man is dead—but, of course, the check *could* have been presented and cashed the morning of the next day. As I understand it, they didn't find Lamont's body until after noon. Get busy there at the bank. If someone showed up with the five-hundred-dollar check and they turned it down because Loring Lamont was dead, they'll remember the occasion and remember the person. If the check was cashed in the morning before they were notified of Loring Lamont's death, the canceled check will be in Lamont's account.''

Drake nodded. ''I'll get on it right away, Perry.''

''And in the meantime,'' Mason said, ''probably before we get all this information, we'll have a chance to go into court and question the witnesses for the prosecution. At least we'll find out what they know about it and what hole card Hamilton Burger, the district attorney, is holding.''

''You think he has an ace in the hole?'' Drake asked.

''He has something.'' Mason said. ''He's altogether too

confident and he's moving altogether too rapidly. There's some bit of evidence in the case that we don't know about, and you can be pretty certain it's evidence that isn't going to do Arlene Ferris any good.''

Drake said, ''You know, Perry, my idea is that her best bet is to show that she was deliberately enticed out there, to use that distributor part to show that the whole thing was deliberately planned by Loring Lamont, and then claim self-defense and . . .''

''Self-defense with a knife wound in the back?'' Mason asked.

''Oh-oh, I stubbed my toe on that one before—'' Drake said.

''The trouble is,'' Mason told him, ''that she's already told her story.''

''She could change it,'' Drake pointed out, ''particularly if she said that she didn't tell the *whole* truth because some of the details would be embarrassing.''

Mason's face was granite hard. ''Whenever she tells her story on the witness stand, Paul, it'll be the truth. It won't be the story that's the most expedient. I think that the truth is not only the most powerful weapon, but as far as I'm concerned it's the only weapon.''

''Have it your way,'' Drake said, ''but she *could* show a little cheesecake and breeze through this case in a walk if she told a story of enticement and used that part from the distributor to back up her claim.''

''Don't worry,'' Mason said, ''we'll use that part from the distributor.''

''But it won't have a real kick unless—well, you know, a girl fighting for her honor and all that.''

''I know,'' Mason said, ''but also don't forget that she told the police they left the ham and eggs untouched and the autopsy shows that Loring Lamont was killed within a matter of minutes after he had eaten those ham and eggs.''

Drake heaved a long sigh. ''Damn it,'' he said, ''someone is always taking the joy out of life.''

Chapter 10

Donald Enders Carson, a young, aggressive trial deputy of the district attorney's office, said, "If the Court please, this is the preliminary hearing of the People of the State of California against Arlene Ferris. The People are ready. The defendant, represented by Perry Mason, is in court, and this is the time heretofore fixed for the preliminary hearing."

"The defendant is ready," Perry Mason said.

"Call your first witness," Judge Carleton Bayton said to the prosecuting attorney.

"Dr. Harmon C. Draper, the autopsy surgeon, will be my first witness," Carson said.

Draper came forward, was sworn, qualified himself, and testified that he had examined the body of Loring Lamont, that death had been caused by a stab wound in the back with a knife which still protruded from the back at the time the body was delivered to the autopsy room; that he could not definitely fix the time of death with reference to the hour of the day, but he could definitely fix death as having occurred within a very few minutes of the time a meal consisting of ham and eggs had been ingested, probably within much less than twenty minutes of the time of the meal, certainly no more than twenty minutes. That death might have taken place at any time after seven or before midnight on the evening of the fifth of the month, but was within twenty minutes of the time the food had been ingested, probably within five to ten minutes of the time the decedent had started to eat the meal.

"Cross-examine," Carson said to Mason.

"*You* have no information as to when the meal was ingested?" Mason asked.

"No."

"Death was instantaneous?"

"Virtually instantaneous."

"Despite the fact that the knife was in the back, Doctor, would it have been possible for the wound to have been inflicted by someone standing in front of the decedent?"

"I think not."

"Thank you," Mason said. "That's all, Doctor."

Carson said to the Court, "I apologize for putting on Dr. Draper out of order. He is, however, exceedingly busy and I told him I would call him as my first witness. I will now proceed with the regular groundwork of showing the location of the crime and the identification of the corpse."

Carson called a surveyor and a photographer, introduced maps, diagrams, sketches and photographs. He then said, "Call Mr. George Quincy Albert."

George Albert took the witness stand.

"If the Court please," Carson said, "I desire to use Mr. Albert as a general witness in this case, and, therefore, in order to save time, I am also going to use him as the witness who will identify the corpse."

"Very well," Judge Bayton said, "let's move along as rapidly as possible, gentlemen. I understand this is a case which has attracted considerable public interest, but, after all, this is simply a preliminary hearing."

"What is your occupation, Mr. Albert?" Carson asked.

"I am now, and for several years have been, an office manager in the executive offices of the Lamont Rolling, Casting and Engineering Company."

"Your age?"

"Thirty-two."

Were you acquainted with Loring Lamont in his lifetime?"

"I was."

"Where is he now?"

"He is dead."

"How do you know he is dead?"

"I identified his body in the morgue."

"Who asked you to do that?"

"The police. They wanted someone to make an identification and it was agreed that since Mr. Jarvis P. Lamont, the father, was quite broken up . . ."

"Never mind that," Carson interrupted. "You made the identification at the request of the police?"

"Yes, sir."

"And that identification was made while you were conferring with the police and the district attorney on the evening of the sixth?"

"Yes, sir."

"The police had sent for you to get information concerning certain phases of the case, and while you were there you volunteered to make the identification of the body at the morgue?"

"Yes, sir."

"You are acquainted with the defendant in this case?"

"Yes, sir."

"How long have you known her?"

"Since she started work at the Lamont Company."

"How long ago was that?"

"A period of a little more than two months."

"Now, directing your attention to the evening of the fifth, which was on Monday, did you have any conversation with the defendant on that day?"

"Yes, sir."

"When?"

"In the evening, after the regular quitting time."

"And what was the conversation? What did she say?"

"There were matters to be taken care of which called for overtime work—that is, it was not a necessity that she work overtime—I very seldom request that of any employee, particularly in view of what might be called a general trend of the times. Stenographers are not as interested now as . . ."

"Never mind that," Carson interrupted. "I am simply asking you if there was a conversation about her working overtime."

"Well, it came time for the office to be closed, that is, for the stenographers to leave and . . ."

"What time is that?"

"Five o'clock."

"And what happened?"

"The defendant kept right on working."

"Did you have a conversation with her?"

"I did later."

"When was that? That is, about what time?"

"About five-thirty. I thanked her for staying to finish the work and she told me that she knew the specifications on which she was working should go in the night's mail, that it was important that they go out and that she had decided to stay and finish them."

"What time did she leave?"

"A little after five-thirty."

"Was anyone else in the office at that time?"

"No, sir. Just the defendant and myself."

"Do you know what the weather was on that night?"

"It was raining. It had been raining during the day."

"You may cross-examine," Carson said.

Mason studied the witness thoughtfully. "You say the defendant had been working for the company for about two months?"

"Yes."

"Had you known her prior to the time she started work?"

"I had not."

"There is a personnel placement department in the corporation?"

"There is."

"And stenographic staff usually comes from this personnel placement?"

"It does."

"Do you have anything to do with hiring the people?"

"I do not."

"But you have authority to discharge them?"

"I do."

"You remember when the defendant started working for you?"

"Very well."

"Did she come to you through the regular placement channels?"

"She did not."

"She was not hired in the ordinary course of employment?"

"She was not. She was placed on the payroll because of specific instructions from Loring Lamont."

Mason straightened in his chair. "You mean that her employment did not go through the regular channels?"

"That is exactly what I mean."

"When did the defendant cease working?"

"I discharged her on the sixth because . . ."

"Answer the question," Mason interrupted. "I am only interested in the date she ceased working for the company."

"The sixth."

"Very well," Mason said. "That concludes my cross-examination."

"No questions on redirect," Carson said.

"Call your next witness," Judge Bayton said to Carson.

"Jerome Henley," Carson announced.

Henley came forward, took the oath, and testified as to his name, residence and occupation.

"Directing your attention to the late evening of the fifth of this month, a Monday evening," Carson said, "I will ask you where you were on that evening."

"In my apartment."

"What is the address of your apartment?"

"9612 Endicott Way."

"That is an apartment house?"

"It is."

"You have an apartment there?"

"I do."

"Are you married or single?"

"Single."

"You live alone in this apartment?"

"I do."

"Are you acquainted with Mr. Loring Lamont, or, rather, were you acquainted with him in his lifetime?"

"I was . . . that is, I'd seen him often enough to know who he was."

"Were you acquainted with the automobile that he drove?"

"I was."

"And I believe he had an apartment in the same apartment house in which you reside?"

"That is right."

"Now, on the evening of the fifth, sometime during the night, did you see someone in Loring Lamont's automobile?"

"I did."

"Do you know who that person was?"

"Yes."

"Who was it?"

"Miss Arlene Ferris, the defendant in this case."

"And what did she do at that date and at that time that you noticed in particular?"

"She had just driven Mr. Loring Lamont's car up to the curb and parked it in front of a fireplug . . . now, just a moment, I will retract that. I *assume* that she drove it up. I walked along just as she was getting out of the car."

"Where was the car parked?"

"Directly in front of a fireplug."

"Did you recognize the car?"

"I did."

"And you recognized the defendant?"

"I did."

"Is there any question in your mind as to the identification?"

"There is none."

"You may inquire," Carson said to Mason.

"You remember the occasion when I entered your store on the seventh?" Mason asked.

"I do, very well indeed, Mr. Mason."

"I was accompanied by a young woman on that occasion?"

"You were."

"And Lieutenant Tragg of Homicide entered your place of business while I was there?"

"He did."

"And he asked you if you had ever seen the young woman who accompanied me on that occasion?"

"That is right."

84

"And did you not, at that time and place in the presence of Lieutenant Tragg and myself and this other woman, state definitely and positively that this other woman was the woman you had seen getting out of the car that night in front of the apartment house?"

"That is correct, I did. I was mistaken."

"The matter was more fresh in your recollection at that time than it is now?"

"No. The contrary is the case—I have had an opportunity to think the entire situation over and I realize now that I was tricked."

"Tricked by whom?"

"By you and by a private detective who showed me a photograph of the young woman who was with you, a woman named Madge Elwood. The circumstances were such that I was forced to associate the photograph with the person I had seen getting out of the car. The power of suggestion was such that when I saw the person who had posed for the picture I made a mistake."

"But you did identify Madge Elwood at that time as the person you had seen parking the car?"

"I repeat, I was tricked into . . ."

"The question is, Did you or did you not make such identification?"

"I did, but it was the result of trickery."

"You did make such identification?"

"Well . . . yes."

"A positive identification?"

"I'm not certain I know what you mean by a positive identification."

"You said you were positive?"

"I may have."

"*Were* you positive of the identification?"

"I thought I was at the time."

"Positive?"

"Mistakenly positive."

"But positive?"

"Well, yes."

"And what date was this that you saw someone parking Lamont's car?"

"It was on the evening of the fifth."

"At what time?"

"I can't tell the exact time."

"Can you tell the approximate time?"

"No, sir, I can't. It was prior to midnight. That's all I know."

"How are you certain it was prior to midnight?"

"Because the place where I got a cup of coffee closes at midnight. I can't be certain as to the time. My watch was at the jeweler's. I had been listening to records and reading. I went sound asleep on the couch. I don't know how long I slept. I wakened and went down to get a cup of coffee. I came back and got into bed. I am not going to testify as to the *exact* time because I don't know. All I can say is that it was some time during the evening of the fifth. I have an impression it was around ten o'clock, but I don't *know*. I just had a sort of ten o'clock feeling, as though I had been sound asleep for three hours. That, of course, is not any evidence, any satisfactory criterion. I must have gone to sleep right after supper. I simply don't know the time."

"What did the defendant do after she got out of the car?"

"She stood at the curb for a minute, turned around and slammed the door shut on the right-hand side of the car. Then she walked down toward the corner."

"Which corner?"

"The corner to the north."

"No further questions," Mason said.

"No redirect examination," Carson said. "My next witness is Thomas Grimes."

Grimes came forward and was sworn, gave his name and address.

"You are employed as a guard in the parking lot at the executive division of the Lamont Rolling, Casting and Engineering Company?"

"I am."

"And is it your duty to check the cars that go in and out?"

86

"Principally to check the cars that go in, but we keep an eye on things."

"You were so employed on the evening of the fifth of this month?"

"I was."

"Were you acquainted with Loring Lamont during his lifetime?"

"Yes, sir. I knew him by sight."

"You were acquainted with his automobile?"

"Yes, sir."

"I will ask you if, on the evening of the fifth, you saw Mr. Loring Lamont leave the parking place in question."

"I did."

"At what time?"

"At approximately five-forty-five."

"Was he alone?"

"He was not."

"Who was with him?"

"A young woman."

"Could you identify that young woman?"

"Yes."

"Is she in court?"

"She is."

"Where?"

"She is the defendant, Arlene Ferris, sitting next to Mr. Perry Mason."

"You may inquire," Carson said, with a slight bow at Mason.

"You're certain this woman was the defendant?" Mason asked.

"I am."

"Do you remember being asked to look at another young woman on the seventh of this month?"

"I do."

"And didn't you identify her as being the woman you saw in Loring Lamont's automobile?"

"I did not," the witness said vehemently. "I did absolutely no such thing. I told Lieutenant Tragg and I told you that I couldn't be sure she was the same one—she wasn't."

"When did you find out she wasn't?"

"After I saw the right young woman."

"Meaning the defendant?"

"Yes."

"And prior to that time you didn't identify this other person as being the one you had seen?"

"I definitely did not. I refused to make the identification. I refused to do so for you and I refused to do so for Lieutenant Tragg."

"Quite right," Mason said. "Did you tell Lieutenant Tragg you weren't certain?"

"I told him I wasn't certain."

"And you weren't certain?"

"Not when I saw Miss Elwood—not that time."

"For how long did you see this woman who was in the car with Loring Lamont?"

"While he was driving through the gate."

"At what speed was he driving?"

"Oh, perhaps ten or twelve miles an hour."

"It was raining?"

"Yes."

"You were under shelter?"

"Yes."

"You were looking through a window in that shelter?"

"Yes."

"So you only saw this young woman while Loring Lamont was driving past that window. That window is how wide?"

"Oh, perhaps thirty inches."

"So you got a glimpse of this young woman while she was moving past a window thirty inches wide at a speed of ten miles an hour?"

"Yes."

"Was this young woman sitting on the left-hand side of the car?"

"Certainly not. Mr. Lamont was driving the car. She was seated on his right."

"You saw Mr. Lamont?"

"Yes."

"You are positive he was driving the car?"

"Positive."

"You didn't look at his face?"

"Of course I looked at his face."

"For how long?"

"Long enough to recognize him."

"While he was driving by?"

"Yes."

"And did you look at the woman before you recognized Loring Lamont or afterwards?"

"Afterwards."

"Then you looked at Loring Lamont first?"

"Yes, sir."

"Now, let's see," Mason said. "If Lamont was driving past a thirty-inch window at ten miles an hour he was going approximately fourteen feet a second, so he drove past the window in approximately one-fifth of a second."

"I haven't figured it out."

"Well, take a pencil and paper and figure it out for yourself," Mason said. "We'll wait."

The witness took a notebook for his pocket, started multiplying, dividing, then nodded his head.

"So you saw the people in the car for approximately one-fifth of a second."

"Yes, sir."

"And in that time you first looked at Loring Lamont long enough to recognize him?"

"Yes, sir."

"Then after that you looked at the person who was with him?"

"Well, I guess so."

"So you looked at this person for less than one-fifth of a second."

"All right."

"And when you saw this other woman on the seventh you said you weren't certain. Isn't that right?"

"That's right."

"You weren't certain that she *was* the woman?"

"That's right."

"And you weren't certain that she *wasn't* the woman?"

89

"I didn't say that she wasn't. However, I didn't think . . ."

"What did you say?"

"I said I wasn't certain."

"That she wasn't the woman?"

"I said I wasn't certain that she *was* the woman."

"You weren't certain that she was *not* the woman?"

"No."

"You simply said you weren't certain?"

"Yes. That's the general effect of it."

"Then after you saw a photograph of the defendant, and after Lieutenant Tragg or some other person on the police force had told you that that picture was one of the woman you saw on the seventh, you became certain?"

"I am now absolutely certain in my own mind that this defendant was the young woman I saw in the car," the witness said.

"Then," Mason said, smiling, "you are certain *now* but you weren't certain on the seventh?"

"I didn't see the defendant on the seventh."

"But you saw another young woman and said you weren't certain that she was not the woman?"

"I wasn't certain."

"Thank you," Mason said. "That's all."

"No questions on redirect," Carson said. "My next witness is Otto Keswick."

Keswick, in his early forties, alert, broad-shouldered, powerful in build, took the stand, was sworn and testified that he lived in a rented room in a house about two miles from the lodge where the murder had been committed, that he was employed as gardener and general handy man, that he had what he described as a somewhat ancient and battered automobile with which he went back and forth to work, that he had no particular hours of employment but was, rather, obligated simply to keep the premises in shape; that sometimes he worked as much as ten or twelve hours a day and other times he worked only a few hours a day.

He further testified that at a little after one o'clock on the afternoon of the sixth he had driven to the lodge, that he had found the outer gate locked with a padlock to which he had the key, that he had inserted the key, unlocked the padlock, driven his car into the grounds, locking the gate behind him in accordance with his instructions, and had started doing some watering and trimming some trees; that he had noticed the side door of the house was slightly ajar, that he had gone to the door to close it, had looked inside and had seen a man's feet lying on the floor, that he had therefore stepped inside to see what was the trouble and had found the body of Loring Lamont.

The witness testified that he had been careful to touch nothing, that he had carefully backed out of the room—had, however, taken the precaution of closing the door; that he had then gone directly to his car, had driven to the gate, unlocked the padlock, gone out, locked the gate behind him and had driven to the home of Sadie Richmond; that he had reported what he had found there and that Mrs. Richmond had telephoned the authorities.

"Your witness," Carson said to Mason.

"How long had you been employed as caretaker and general handy man prior to the murder?" Mason asked.

"For about two years."

"You knew the various persons who used the lodge and they were acquainted with you—I am referring now to the executives of the company?"

"Yes, sir."

"You knew J. P. Lamont?"

"Yes, sir."

"And he knew you?"

"Of course."

"And you knew Loring Lamont?"

"Certainly."

"Quite well?" Mason asked.

"I knew him as well as could be expected, and he knew me."

"When Mr. J. P. Lamont called you to do anything, what did he call you? How did he address you?"

"Otto."

"When Loring Lamont called you, what did he call you?"

"Otto."

"Did Mr. Loring Lamont ever refer to you by your initials of O.K.?"

The witness hesitated for an all but imperceptible moment, then said, "Not to my knowledge. He called me Otto."

"Where were you the night of the fifth?" Mason asked.

"I was at home."

"And where is at home?"

"At the residence I mentioned, where I rent a room."

"Was anyone else with you?"

"Not with me, but I was with someone."

"Who?"

"Mrs. Arthur Sparks."

"And who is Mrs. Sparks?"

"She is a widowed woman of about sixty-five. She owns the place where I rent a room. I was with her in the living room at her request, watching television."

"During what time?"

"From about seven o'clock in the evening until ten-thirty."

"About ten-thirty?"

"Exactly ten-thirty," the witness said. "The television show I was watching was over at ten-thirty and as soon as the show was over I went to bed."

"What time did you get up in the morning?"

"About seven-thirty."

"But you didn't go to the lodge until a little after one o'clock?"

"That's right. I did some odd jobs around the house for Mrs. Sparks. I don't pay cash rental for my room, but keep the house and grounds in order."

"Are you paid a salary for taking care of the lodge?"

"No, sir. I am paid by the hour. I put in the time I think necessary and keep track of my time and am paid by the hour."

"Who checks on your time—anyone? Do they simply put you on your honor?"

"Not exactly. I keep an account of my time and give Sadie Richmond my time slips. She marks them 'O.K.' and puts them in the desk. Then someone from the company picks them up, figures the total of hours and the total I have coming and they send out a check.''

''You're certain the gate was locked when you went to the place on the sixth?''

''Quite certain.''

''Was there anything at all about the premises that indicated anything unusual had taken place there?''

''Only the door which was standing slightly ajar.''

''Nothing else?''

''Nothing else.''

''Thank you,'' Mason said. ''That's all.''

Keswick left the stand, quite evidently relieved that his cross-examination had been so perfunctory.

Carson said, ''My next witness, if the Court please, is Peter Lyons. I think his testimony will be rather brief.''

Judge Bayton glanced at the clock. ''Let us hope so,'' he said. ''This is only a preliminary hearing, yet it has consumed the entire morning. I'm afraid it will be necessary to take the usual noon adjournment. I had hoped to have the afternoon free for another case.''

''Perhaps,'' the prosecutor said, ''counsel will be willing to stipulate to Mr. Lyons' testimony.''

''What do you expect to prove by him?'' Mason asked.

''Mr. Lyons,'' Carson said, ''is a police officer who was on duty until midnight on the night of the fifth. He will testify that he found the automobile of Loring Lamont parked in front of a fireplug, that he issued a ticket for illegal parking. The location of the illegally parked car was exactly where the witness, Jerome Henley, saw it when the young woman emerged from it.''

''Only one ticket was issued?'' Mason asked.

''That's all that this particular officer issued.''

''What eventually became of the car?''

''Other officers who came on duty after midnight tagged the car for illegal parking and eventually, at three o'clock in the morning, it was towed away. Ordinarily these officers do not enforce traffic regulations but there had been trouble with illegal parking in the vicinity and an order had gone out to watch for illegal parking. All officers patrolling this district had been instructed to tag cars, and, after the second or third tag, to have the offending car towed away."

"And I take it," Mason said, "that you have talked with all these officers yourself and understand the facts?"

"I have."

"Upon that statement by counsel," Mason said, "I will stipulate that Officer Lyons, if called, would so testify on direct examination that he gave one tag for illegal parking. At what time was it?"

"About nine. He gave one parking ticket at about nine P.M.," Carson said.

"You know that to be the fact?" Mason asked.

"I do."

"Then I will stipulate that would be his testimony on direct examination."

Carson went on. "And will you stipulate that the other officers who came on duty at midnight gave two additional parking tickets and the car was towed away about three o'clock?"

"You state that as a fact?" Mason asked.

"I do," Carson said. "Not, of course, of my own knowledge but based upon my conversation with the officers."

"I will stipulate that these officers would so testify on direct examination," Mason said.

"Does that conclude your case?" the judge asked.

Carson glanced at the clock and said, "Unfortunately, it does not. I have one other witness I intend to put on the stand."

"His testimony will be brief?" Judge Bayton asked.

"I don't know. That depends quite largely on cross-examination. The witness is Lieutenant Tragg, who will testify to some very significant facts."

"Can they be stipulated?" Judge Bayton asked.

"I am afraid not, Your Honor. These facts are quite—well, I dislike to comment on the evidence in advance, but these facts are quite conclusive, and perhaps may come as a surprise to the defense."

"After all, this is only a preliminary hearing," Judge Bayton said. "There's no jury present. Go ahead and state what you expect to prove."

Carson said, "This witness will testify not only to circumstantial evidence but to conversations with the defendant and admissions made by her. I would prefer to let the witness disclose the circumstantial evidence."

"Very well," Judge Bayton said with obvious reluctance, "we will have to continue the case apparently through the afternoon. Court will adjourn until two o'clock P.M. The defendant is in custody and is remanded to custody."

Arlene Ferris glanced apprehensively at Perry Mason. "How is it coming?" she asked, as the judge retired to his chambers.

"Better than I had expected," Mason said. "Those witnesses are so mixed up in their identification now that by the time we get them in the Superior Court in front of a jury they'll have testified to two different things."

"But that means you expect I'll be bound over for trial in the Superior Court?" she asked apprehensively.

"I'm afraid so," Mason said. "Attorneys seldom expect to have a defendant released at a preliminary hearing—and, after all, young lady, circumstances have conspired to put you behind the legal eight ball."

"I hadn't realized what a nightmare this would be," she said, "being shut up in jail and . . . it's horrible."

"No one ever realizes what it means until it happens," Mason told her. "I'm sorry, Arlene, but right now I don't care to try to play things any differently. If I tried to get you released now I might wind up doing your case a lot more harm than good. I'd have to put you on the stand and you'd have to convince the judge you were telling the truth. You can't do that with Judge Bayton. He adopts the position that it's not up to him to judge a conflict in the evidence, that as long as there's evidence indicating a crime and connecting the defendant with the commission of that crime, he binds the defendant over to the Superior Court and lets the jury decide—I think we can get you a quick trial and . . ."

"And then what?" she interrupted.

"And prompt acquittal," Mason said, "if you do *exactly* as I say."

"I'll do it." she promised.

Mason patted her shoulder. "All right, chin up," Mason told her.

She hesitated. "Is it true that Jarvis P. Lamont has said I'm a liar and an adventuress, that he's going to go through my past with a fine-tooth comb?"

"That's true," Mason said. "And it's a wonderful thing in your favor. I'm going to encourage the press to exploit it as much as possible. It's wonderful publicity for you. The picture of a young, virtually penniless woman fighting for her freedom and her honor, and, pitted against her, a ruthless tycoon who is trying to prop up the reputation of a profligate son by damning the woman whom the son wronged, is going to make a background that will arouse public sympathy and the sympathy of a jury. You'll have to go now. Keep a stiff upper lip."

Mason watched Arlene Ferris being led out of the courtroom, then went to the back of the courtroom where Paul Drake and Della Street were chatting with Madge Elwood.

"How does it look?" Madge Elwood asked.

"About the way I expected—perhaps a little better." Mason said. "This Jerome Henley was so mad that he had been tricked, he blurted out some admissions that we can use later."

"Won't he deny he said them?" Madge Elwood asked. "I think he's capable of it."

Mason shook his head. "There's a court reporter taking everything down. What he said is in the record and it's going to stay in the record. We're going out to lunch. Better come along."

"No, thanks. I . . . I have a date with a friend."

"You'll be in court this afternoon?"

"Of course."

"At two o'clock," Mason said. "Be sure to be there."

Mason turned to Paul Drake. "Paul," he said, "there's something peculiar about that car being parked in front of the fireplug."

"What do you mean?"

"This officer, Peter Lyons, tagged the car around nine. He put the first tag on it. Now, Henley saw Arlene Ferris getting out of the car. He can't fix the time but because of the parking ticket we know it must have been before nine.

"Now then, we run into a sort of hiatus. The officers were instructed to watch for illegal parking, to put on two or three tags and then radio for a tow-car. Lyons went off duty at twelve o'clock, he put the first tag on the car at nine o'clock. The other two officers came on at midnight. They found the car illegally parked and put two or three tags on it, and then had it towed away. But what happened between nine o'clock and midnight? Why didn't Lyons tag it again?"

Drake shrugged his shoulders. "Those things can happen."

"Well," Mason said, "I've offered to stipulate, but there's a string to my offer Carson may not have noticed. Get a couple of operatives checking the records at police headquarters. Let's see what happened to that car—just how many tags were on it and when they were put on it."

Drake said, "Why didn't you bring out the fact that Otto Keswick had a criminal record, Perry? You could have shown him up on cross-examination."

"Sure," Mason said. "I could have done that all right, and it would have harmed Keswick, but wouldn't have done our case a darned bit of good. There's no use dragging out a man's dead past unless you expect to accomplish something by doing it.

"Incidentally, Paul, just check his alibi. Ask this Mrs. Sparks if he's correct on his time of watching the television—better send a man out there to talk with her and have him phone in a report."

"Okay," Drake said, moving toward the phone booth. "You and Della have lunch and I'll get busy on the phone and try to line up the information you want."

As Drake entered the phone booth, a short, heavy-set man of about forty-five came pushing purposefully through the last of the spectators who were straggling from the courtroom.

Cold gray eyes beneath black eyebrows surveyed Mason. "Perry Mason?"

Mason nodded.

The man's hands were pushed down in the side pockets of his coat. He kept them there. "Orval Kingman," he said.

"Oh, yes," Mason observed.

"In my business," Kingman said, "a man keeps an eye on his back trail. If anyone starts sniffing around he wants to know why. He also wants to know who and then he may want to do something about it."

Mason stood looking down at the man, at the hands thrust in the side pockets, the belligerent set of the shoulders.

"And so?" Mason asked.

"And so," Kingman said, "I get the word that private eyes are sniffing around on my trail. Then I get the word that these private eyes are employed by Perry Mason and that you might have the idea of dragging my name into this Lamont murder case."

"And so?" Mason asked.

"And so I came to tell you not to do it."

Mason said, "When I'm trying a case nobody tells me what to do and what not to do. I do the thing that's for the best interests of my client. You're a bookmaker. Loring Lamont played the horses with you. You evidently had some kind of an understanding with him by which he played on the cuff until the amount reached five hundred dollars, then you collected."

"All right," Kingman said. "That still doesn't mean you can make me a patsy in order to get your client out of a jam."

"I'm not trying to make you a patsy," Mason said. "I'm trying to get at the facts. If I find the facts will benefit my client I'll bring them out in court."

"Now that just might not be healthy," Kingman said.

"For you or for me?"

"For you, Mr. Mason."

"I'll watch out for my health," Mason said. "It's excellent, thank you. You can watch out for yours. Now, suppose you tell me what you were doing on the night of the fifth."

"That I'll do," Kingman said. "That's one of things I came to tell you."

"It might have helped the situation if you'd told me first," Mason said, "instead of discussing my health."

Kingman shrugged his shoulders, set his thick neck, looked up at Mason and said, "I was in a poker game."

"From when until when?"

"From seven o'clock until nearly midnight."

"That can be established?" Mason asked.

"That can be established," Kingman said, "but the people who were playing with me wouldn't want to have their names brought into it."

"You got a check from Loring Lamont on the fifth?"

"On the morning of the fifth."

"What time?"

"About ten o'clock, I guess."

"To cover past bets?"

"Let's put it this way—it kept his credit up."

"You didn't trust him for more than five hundred dollars?"

"Look, Mr. Mason, I don't trust anyone for more than five hundred dollars. That's my limit."

"He made bets on the fifth?"

"That's right."

"On the afternoon of the fifth?"

"On the afternoon of the fifth."

"And won or lost?"

"Does that make any difference?"

"I think it does, because I think perhaps he lost rather heavily and you wanted five hundred dollars more from him before you got in that poker game."

"Aren't you funny!" Kingman said sarcastically.

"And," Mason said, "you telephoned him and told him he'd been plunging and had gone over the five hundred credit limit, that you wanted five hundred and that you were coming out to collect it. You probably told him you were going to sit in a poker game that night and you wanted cash."

"That would be a nice idea," Kingman said. "Go ahead, follow it up. What happened after that?"

"You went out to the lodge."

"All the way out there to collect a lousy five hundred bucks?"

"You may have needed it. You were going to be sitting in a poker game. I don't imagine they took IOU's in that poker game."

"Okay," Kingman said. "Keep talking, Counselor. Let's get this idea of yours out in the open and look it over. You think I went out there to collect the five hundred bucks."

"You could have."

"And then what?"

"You could have had an argument and stuck a knife in his back."

"You mean I took a knife out there with me?"

"There were knives in the kitchen."

"So I went out there, had a talk with him about five hundred bucks and stuck a knife into him?"

"I'm simply investigating the possibilities," Mason said.

"All right. Let's look at it this way," Kingman said. "Why would I stick a knife in him? He was a customer."

"Perhaps because he didn't pay the five hundred bucks."

The black bushy eyebrows went up. "Loring Lamont didn't pay the five hundred? Come, come, Counselor, you're going to have to do better than that. Loring Lamont wanted to keep his credit good with me. He liked to play the horses and I was his bookie. He knew he could trust me. I paid off when he won. I kept my mouth shut. The old man was never going to learn anything about what was going on through me. Loring Lamont knew that. Why should he refuse to pay me the five hundred bucks?"

"Perhaps he gave you a check," Mason said, watching the man closely.

"All right, go on. What happened?"

"And then you got in an argument—perhaps over a woman."

"How you talk," Kingman said. "Look, Mr. Mason, in my type of business women grow on bushes."

"This may have been a particular woman."

"Not with me. There aren't any particular women. In my

100

racket a broad is a broad. Now let's get this thing straight,"
Kingman said. "You think I went out there to collect five
hundred bucks because I was going to get in a poker game.
You think I was in a hurry for the five hundred smackeroos."

"It could be," Mason said.

"Sure, it could be," Kingman said, with a twisted smile
which emphasized the line of his broken nose. "So I went
out to get the five hundred. Then, in place of hurrying back
to a poker game, Loring Lamont said, 'Look, Orval, I had
a date with a babe who ran out on me. We were just getting
ready to sit down and eat some ham and eggs. They're getting
a little cold now, but why don't you sit down here with me
and have some ham and eggs?'

"So I sat down at the table with him and had some cold
ham and eggs, notwithstanding the fact I was in a hurry to
get back to this poker game."

"You seem to know a lot about what happened," Mason
said.

"In my business, when someone tries to frame me for
something, I find out the facts."

"All right," Mason said. "You find out the facts. Now
I'll tell you what might have happened. Lamont might have
told you, 'Look, Orval, I'm hungry. This food is on the table.
I was just sitting down to eat when a babe ran out on me.
You wait until I've finished eating and I'll make you out a
check. If you're hungry you can eat that plate of ham and
eggs. If you aren't, you can throw them out.'"

"Okay," Kingman said. "We'll ride along with it your
way, Counselor. Then what happened?"

"Then you ate the ham and eggs and then you had an
argument."

"Did I get a check or didn't I?"

"You got a check," Mason said.

"For five hundred bucks?"

"For five hundred bucks."

"And then I got in an argument with him?"

"That's the part I'm investigating."

"Go ahead and investigate all you damn please," Kingman said. "For your information, Mr. Mason, I didn't go

101

out to that country place. I didn't call him on the telephone. I only got the one check from him and that was in the morning. You'll find that I cashed it at the bank before two o'clock. That was on the fifth. I don't hound my customers and when I want to play poker I don't have to go dashing around getting money to put up for an ante. Now, you have a theory. You'd better get some facts to back up your theory before you start making it public."

"Don't tell me how to practice law," Mason said. And then added quietly, "Now you've been telling me things. I'm going to tell you something. I'm investigating this case. I have no desire to try to push anyone around. I don't want to invade anyone's private life. I want to know what happened, that's all. You say you were in a poker game from seven until nearly midnight. Give me the names of the people you were playing with. I'll check. It will be a quiet check. If you check out, that's all there is to it. If you don't, I'll do some more checking."

"I've told you some of these people wouldn't want to be brought into it."

"That may be," Mason said, "but there are certain facts which lead me to believe you may have talked on the telephone with Loring Lamont."

"What facts?"

"Let me ask you this," Mason said. "How did he refer to you? Did he call you by your first name or by your initials?"

"By my first name, whenever he used names. If he called me anything he'd call me Orval."

"He never called you O.K.?"

"He never called me O.K.," the man said, the gray eyes holding Mason's.

"All right," Mason said. "Give me a list of the persons who were in the game with you and I'll check. I'll do it quietly."

Kingman shook his head. "I tell you, I don't do business that way. I'm telling you what the facts are for your own guidance, just so you don't lead with your chin and so you keep healthy."

Mason reached to an inside pocket, pulled out a folded legal document, took out his fountain pen, wrote the name "Orval Kingman" in a blank and handed the document to Kingman.

"What's this?" the man asked, unfolding the paper to look at it.

"That," Mason said, "is a subpoena duly issued under the seal of the court, ordering you to appear at two o'clock this afternoon as a witness on behalf of the defense."

Kingman's face darkened. "I've tried to tell you and tell you nice," he said.

"And I've tried to tell you and tell you nice," Mason told him. "You give me a list of the men who were in that poker game with you and I'll check. Otherwise, you'll go on the stand and tell where you were on the night of the fifth."

"You're bluffing," Kingman said. "You aren't going to put on any evidence. No smart lawyer ever puts on evidence on behalf of the defense at a preliminary hearing."

Mason shrugged his shoulders. "You've got your subpoena. Be there at two o'clock this afternoon. If you think I'm bluffing this will be a good way to find out."

"Now, wait a minute," Kingman said. "Let's not get each other wrong. I . . ."

"You have your subpoena," Mason said. "If you want to get out of testifying temporarily you can give me a list of those names."

Kingman's face darkened, then abruptly he pulled a notebook from his pocket, started writing.

"There are five names," he said, tearing the sheet from the notebook and handing it to Mason. "Those people wouldn't like it if they thought I'd given you the information. But if you want to check with them quietly and confidentially you'll find out where I was on the night of the fifth.

"There are two men whose names I've marked with a little check mark. I'd prefer to have you start with them. They're regular poker players and it wouldn't mean so much to them. The other three men are businessmen who think they're pretty good poker players."

"They lost?" Mason asked.

"As it happens, they lost."

"And you won and these two men whose names you have checked won?"

"If it's any of your business, we won."

"I can see why you might not care to have the situation publicized," Mason said.

"That doesn't make me guilty of murder, Mr. Mason."

"Now there," Mason told him, "is where you're using words that I'll listen to. I don't want to abuse my position or the power of the law. All I'm interested in is finding out what happened. If you were in that poker game and didn't leave it, that's enough for me. Even if you can't prove an alibi I'll still do some checking before I put you on the stand or bring your name into it—assuming, of course, that you don't start calling my hand. If you want to call my hand we'll start putting cards on the table."

Kingman said, "Okay, Counselor, that's good enough for me. They told me you were a square shooter. Get your men doing a little investigating and you'll find I'm clean."

Abruptly the man's right hand shot out of his pocket and was extended toward Mason.

Mason shook hands.

"They told me you were on the up and up," Kingman said. "I just had to be sure, that's all."

"You only got the one check that day?" Mason asked.

"So help me, Counselor, that's the truth. I got the one check. I saw him about ten o'clock in the morning when he stopped by to give me the check and he picked some horses for the afternoon. And since we're putting cards on the table, I'll tell you something else. He won. Not too heavy, but he won. If he'd lived he would have had money coming to him."

"And as it is?"

"As it is, he gets nothing," Kingman said. "That's one of the chances a man takes. If I give him credit and he bets with me, loses and then drops dead I can't present a bill against his estate. If he bets with me and wins and drops dead his estate doesn't get anything. I can't come in and say, 'I'm a bookie. I owe the guy fifteen hundred bucks.' "

"Was it that much?" Mason asked.

"Just about," Kingman said.

He turned to Della Street. "I'm sorry I had to strut my stuff in front of you, Miss Street," he said, "but with a man like Mason you have to talk to him when you can get him. I didn't know what he was planning to do this afternoon and I wanted to talk with him—I'm glad I did."

He bowed, swung on his heel and pounded his way back down the corridor toward the elevators.

Mason glanced at Della Street.

"Well," she said.

"What's the reaction of your feminine intuition?" Mason asked.

"I believe him," she said. "That last touch was the thing that sold me. When he said that Loring Lamont had won and if he lived he'd have had some money coming to him."

Mason nodded thoughtfully. "Just the same," he said, "we'll get hold of Paul Drake and do a little checking on that poker game. That five-hundred-dollar check to a person listed simply as 'O.K.' assumes even greater importance as we go on."

"Of course," Della Street pointed out, "the initials 'O.K.' wouldn't necessarily be those of the person receiving the check. It could be some sort of a code."

"In which event," Mason said, "it's up to us to crack the code. Come on, Della, let's eat."

Chapter 11

At five minutes before two o'clock, as Mason was entering the courtroom, Paul Drake, hurrying from a telephone booth, tapped the lawyer on the shoulder.

"What is it, Paul?"

"Everything checks on that car in front of the fireplug," Drake Said. "Peter Lyons, who went off duty about midnight, gave the first ticket. After midnight there were two more tickets. Police had been ordered to keep a watch on that street. They'd been troubled with a lot of illegal parking there and had had lots of complaints about blocked driveways, so orders had gone out to keep an eye on cars in the district, tag on the first illegal parking, then keep an eye on the car and order a tow-away after the third ticket.

"The Lamont car was handled as routine until police found out about its importance. By that time the car had been towed away. Of course, after the murder there was a frantic scramble to look the car over for fingerprints. I think they have some."

Mason thought that statement over.

"Well?" Drake asked. "Does that hit you too hard?"

"I don't know," Mason said. "We'll see what develops."

The lawyer walked on into the courtroom.

When Judge Bayton had called court to order, Mason said, "If the Court please, I was asked to stipulate to the testimony of the officers about the parked car.

"I am, of course, willing to make any stipulations which will save time and which do not affect the substantial rights of the defendant. However, in regard to the testimony of Peter Lyons, the officer who put the first tag on the car at nine o'clock, I feel that the interests of the defendant require I should cross-examine the officer. I am therefore serving notice on the prosecution at this time that, while I was willing to stipulate as to what Lyons' testimony would have been on direct examination, I now wish to exercise my right of cross-examination."

"Very well," Judge Bayton said. "That was the stipulation, and I presume the prosecution will have Officer Lyons here for cross-examination, although the Court doesn't see that the testimony in regard to the parked car has any great significance."

Donald Carson arose with smiling urbanity. "Not only do I agree with Your Honor, but since it now appears his testimony would necessitate a delay in the case, I will withdraw my stipulation and we won't use the testimony of Officer Lyons at all."

"Then you withdraw your stipulation as to Lyons' testimony and it will be considered he was not a witness?" Judge Bayton asked.

"Yes, Your Honor."

"Just a minute, if the Court please," Mason said, getting to his feet. "We object to such procedure. Officer Lyons, having been brought into the case, can't be taken out of it now. The understanding was that I would stipulate as to his testimony on direct examination. The defense has the right of cross-examination."

"But the prosecution has now withdrawn the witness," Judge Bayton said.

"The prosecution can't do it," Mason said, "after I accepted the stipulation. Officer Lyons was deemed to have testified on direct examination that certain things happened. This was subject to my right of cross-examination in the event I desired to use that right. The stipulation was offered, was accepted and I desire to use the right of cross-examination."

Judge Bayton frowned. "Is it *that* important, Mr. Mason?"

"I don't know," Mason admitted frankly, "but I intend to find out."

"Very well," Judge Bayton said, smiling. "I think Mr. Mason is correct, Mr. Prosecutor. The stipulation was offered and was accepted. The defense has the right to cross-examine any witnesses he so chooses. You will have Mr. Lyons in court."

"I don't know that we can get him in court on such short notice," Carson said.

"But you must have realized that the stipulation was so worded that the defense could cross-examine him if it so desires," Judge Bayton said with some indication of impatience.

"But I didn't have the faintest idea that the defense would want to cross-examine the officer."

"Well, you evidently guessed wrong," Judge Bayton snapped. "The Court trusts you will arrange to have Officer Lyons here for cross-examination so that the case will not be delayed. Now who's your next witness?"

"Lieutenant Tragg of Homicide," Carson said.

"Very well. Put Lieutenant Tragg on the stand and arrange to get Officer Lyons here so he can be cross-examined."

"If I may have the indulgence of the Court for a moment," Carson said with poor grace, "I'll see what can be done about getting Officer Lyons here."

Carson glared at Perry Mason, tiptoed over to an officer, whispered briefly to him, then straightened and said, "Lieutenant Tragg to the stand, please."

Lt. Tragg, broad-shouldered, grizzled, lumbered up to the witness stand, was sworn, gave his name, address and occupation and faced Carson expectantly.

"You were called to the Chatsworth property of the Lamont Rolling, Casting and Engineering Company on the evening of the sixth?"

"I was."

"And the body of Loring Lamont, which had been previously discovered, was still there at that time?"

"No. The body had been removed before I got there."

"Now, Lieutenant, I don't want to take up a lot of time going over details which are already in evidence, so I will therefore, with the permission of counsel, ask questions which are sufficiently leading to designate the particular evidence I want to elicit. Were you present at the morgue when

108

a search was made of the pockets of the clothing of Loring Lamont?''

"I was.''

"Was anything particularly unusual found in those pockets?''

"Yes.''

"What?''

"A rotating part for the electrical distributing system on an automobile.''

"Do you have that part in your possession at the present time?''

"I do.''

"Will you produce it, please?''

Lt. Tragg reached in his pocket, took out a sealed envelope, took a knife from his pocket, cut through the edge of the envelope, took out a small object and handed it to the deputy district attorney, who, in turn, submitted it to Mason for his inspection, then turned back to the witness.

"What is the function of this part in the distributing system of an automobile, Lieutenant—if you know?''

"It distributes the electrical charge in rotation to the different spark plugs so that the cylinders will fire in order.''

"And if this part is removed from a car, what is the effect on the ignition system?''

"The ignition systems fails. You can't get any current to the spark plugs.''

"And it is, therefore, impossible for the car to operate?''

"That is right. You can't start the motor.''

"And this was found in the pocket of the decedent?''

"It was.''

"Are you familiar with the automobile of the defendant in this case?''

"I am, yes, sir.''

"Can you state whether or not this part, which I now hand to you, fits the electrical system in the car of the defendant?''

"It does.''

Carson turned to Perry Mason and said, "Strictly speaking, the questions I am now going to ask Lieutenant Tragg can be objected to as hearsay, but in the interest of saving time and simply in order to present a complete picture to the Court, I am going to ask these questions, realizing that if counsel for the defense wishes he can object and I will then be forced to put a mechanic on the stand. However, I think we all wish to save time on matters about which there can be no dispute."

Carson turned back to Lt. Tragg. "Did you make any investigation as to whether the car of the defendant had been in a condition to be operated on the night of the fifth?"

"I did."

"What did you find?"

"The car had remained on the parking lot all the night of the fifth and the morning of the sixth. On the morning of the sixth, a mechanic came to the lot, tested the car and repaired it so it would start."

"Do you know what the mechanic found to be wrong with the car?"

"I do."

"What?"

"This part was missing from the distributor."

"This part?"

"Either this part or a part identical with it."

Carson said, "I will now ask that this rotating part be placed in evidence as People's Exhibit—whatever the next designation may be."

"I think it's Exhibit B-7," Judge Bayton said.

"Very well. Let it be marked as Exhibit B-7 for identification."

"Now then, Lieutenant Tragg," Carson went on, turning once more to the witness, "you interrogated the defendant concerning her whereabouts on the evening of the fifth of this month?"

"I did."

"When did that interrogation take place?"

"On the seventh, after the defendant had been picked up by the police."

"Who was present at the time of that conversation?"

"I was and Ralph Grave, a member of the police force."

110

"And were any inducements, threats or promises made to the defendant in order to get her to make a statement?"

"There were none."

"Was she advised as to her rights and the fact that she did not need to make a statement?"

"She was told that any statement she might make could be used against her. I asked her if she cared to explain where she had been on the night of the fifth and whether she had been with Loring Lamont."

"And what did the defendant say?"

"Briefly, she stated that she had tried to start her car in the parking lot, that it would not start, that Loring Lamont had come along and offered her a ride, that he had taken her to the rural lodge maintained by the Lamont Company, that there he had attempted to force his attentions upon her, that this came at a time when he had cooked up a supper of ham and eggs and she had baked biscuits, that she repulsed his advances and ran out of the cabin, down the road; that he had started to follow her in his automobile, so she had detoured to the side of the road and crawled through the barbed wire, that she had then realized he was following her tracks in the wet ground on the surface of the dirt road, that when he came to the place where she had crawled through the wire, he had stopped and left the car with the motor running while he crawled through the fence after her, that she had managed to double back, get through the fence, race down the road and had jumped into the car and taken off in his automobile before he could catch up with the car.

"She further said that she had driven the car back to town and then, feeling that she would add what she called a touch of sardonic humor to the situation, had deliberately parked it in front of a fireplug and had gone off and left it."

"Did she say what time that was?"

"She said she thought it was about eight-fifteen to eight-thirty."

"And she had deliberately parked the car in front of the fireplug?"

"Directly in front of the fireplug."

"Had left the keys in it?"

111

"Yes."

"Now, to go back a moment, she stated to you that the deceased had cooked ham and eggs?"

"That is right."

"Did she state that they had partaken of the ham and eggs?"

"She specifically stated that the altercation had taken place and she had run away prior to the time the ham and eggs were consumed."

"Did you," Carson asked, "make any attempt to verify certain aspects of this statement by physical examination of the evidence and any objects which might tend to furnish corroboration?"

"I did, yes, sir."

"What did you do and what did you find?"

"First we dusted Loring Lamont's car for fingerprints. We found two of the defendant's fingerprints on the back of the rearview mirror. We also searched the road trying to find tracks which would corroborate the statement made by the defendant."

"And what, if anything, did you find?"

"We found that there had been so much travel over the dirt road that it was impossible to detect footprints on the road. Following the discovery of the body, there was an enormous amount of travel due to the nature of the crime and public interest because of the social and financial prominence of the victim."

"That was on the road itself?"

"Yes, sir, that was on the road itself."

"Now, what about the place adjoining the road—the bank?"

Lt. Tragg squared his shoulders as though bracing himself for an attack. "We found," he said, choosing his words carefully, "where the defendant had planted evidence in an attempt to corroborate her story."

Judge Bayton looked up quickly, snapping to attention at the answer. He glanced at Perry Mason, then at Donald Carson, then at the witness.

"Is there any objection to that question or any motion to

strike," he asked, "on the ground the witness has testified to a conclusion?"

Mason said, "Rather than object, I would like to cross-examine the witness on the point."

"You can't sit idly by and let extraneous matter be brought into a case, hoping to cross-examine," Judge Bayton said.

"I don't think it's extraneous," Mason said. "If the defendant did plant this evidence it's a very material and a very convincing fact."

"But the witness doesn't *know* she planted it," Judge Bayton snapped. "I think it's your duty to object and move to strike."

"If the Court please," Carson said, "I think the witness *does* know it. I think the circumstantial evidence on the point is damning. We would welcome cross-examination; both the witness and the prosecution would welcome it."

"Well, it isn't up to the Court to tell counsel how to try his case," Judge Bayton said. "The witness has certainly testified to a conclusion, however."

"A conclusion which I think this witness, by reason of his training as an expert and his peculiar aptitude in such matters, is quite competent to draw," Perry Mason said urbanely. "There is no objection by the defense."

Carson swung back to the question of the witness. "Just what did you find?"

"At first, and on the morning of the seventh, prior to the time we had questioned the defendant, we found that someone had cut a piece from the hem of the defendant's skirt. This piece had been cut with a knife. Then this fragment or segment had been taken out to the barbed-wire fence near the scene of the crime. Someone had impaled it on the barbed-wire fence in such a position that it would be certain to attract attention.

"We then found that some woman, wearing high-heeled shoes, had been lifted against the bank and had been lowered down the soft soil, leaving tracks made by high-heeled shoes in an apparent attempt to make it appear this person had slid through the lower wire of the fence."

"Are you prepared to state definitely, Lieutenant Tragg,

that this person who had left those tracks did *not* slide through under the wire of the fence?"

"Definitely."

"And how can you tell that?"

"Because the ground was sufficiently soft back of the fence to have retained the imprint of heel tracks, and there were no tracks on the other side of the fence—that is, the side away from the road."

"Did you subsequently find the skirt from which that piece had been cut?"

"We did."

"Where?"

"It was one of the defendant's skirts and had been left temptingly displayed in her apartment where it would be virtually impossible to miss it."

"Do you have that skirt with you?"

"I do."

"Will you produce it, please?"

Tragg opened a brief case and produced the skirt Madge Elwood had been wearing when she and Perry Mason visited the apartment of Arlene Ferris.

"You have the piece which was cut from the garment with you?"

"I have."

"Will you produce it, please?"

Tragg produced the torn piece.

"This triangular piece fits in the hem of the garment?"

"It does."

"Will you please demonstrate to the Court?"

Tragg spread the skirt out over his knee, took the triangular piece of cloth which Mason had cut from the garment and fitted it into place.

Judge Bayton, frowning, leaned over from the bench to study the piece of cloth and the skirt with the cut hem, then glanced ominously at Perry Mason.

"Please let the Court inspect that, Lieutenant," he said.

Tragg spread the garment and the torn piece on the bench. Judge Bayton carefully fitted them together.

"We now ask that the skirt and the fragment be introduced

114

in evidence as People's Exhibits, appropriate numbers—B-8 for the skirt, B-9 for the fragment," Carson said.

Judge Bayton said, "Counsel is, of course, entitled to examine this witness on *voir dire* before the articles are introduced in evidence. Does counsel wish to do so?"

"Counsel does," Mason said.

"Very well. You may examine the witness on *voir dire*," Judge Bayton said.

Mason smiled at Lt. Tragg. "You have said that the evidence was designed to substantiate the story of the defendant?"

"There can be no other possible explanation," Tragg said crisply.

Mason smiled. "Then the attempt was rather clumsy, Lieutenant. A person trying to substantiate a story of the defendant would, at least, have had the young woman who was leaving the tracks go on the other side of the fence and run along the soft ground."

"There may not have been time."

"And," Mason went on calmly, "you have stated that the skirt from which this fragment was cut was a skirt belonging to the defendant."

"It was her size and found in her apartment. I consider that sufficient evidence of ownership."

"Did you make any attempt to find where the defendant had purchased this skirt, Lieutenant?"

"No."

"Why?"

"Because I didn't think it was necessary."

"Did you make any attempt to find cleaning marks on the skirt? That is, the identification marks made by cleaners?"

"Yes. We found the code number on the skirt."

"Did you make any attempt to trace that cleaning mark?"

"Not as yet."

"You are aware that different cleaners use different code marks and that those marks are sometimes stamped in indelible inks, sometimes invisible ink which is only visible under ultraviolet light, and that it is possible to trace the ownership of a garment through these figures?"

"That is a technique which is used by the police many times a month."

"But you didn't use it in this case?"

"Not as yet."

"Yet you have testified that this skirt is the property of the defendant?"

"On the evidence we have I still say it is hers. It is her size and it was found in the defendant's apartment."

"Now then," Mason said, "this little bit of cloth hanging from the barbed-wire fence attracted your attention, did it not?"

"It did."

"And caused you to study the tracks carefully?"

"That is right."

"And from that careful study you came to the conclusion that an attempt had been made to furnish what we might call a synthetic corroboration for the story of the defendant?"

Tragg said, "That question calls for my opinion. I will give that opinion. I believe the defendant killed Loring Lamont. There may have been extenuating circumstances, but rather than tell the truth about these circumstances the defendant decided to concoct a story about having been pursued through a barbed-wire fence and deliberately sought to plant evidence which would support her story."

"That's a conclusion of the witness," Judge Bayton pointed out.

"It's his opinion as an expert," Carson insisted. "The question called for it, and his answer was responsive."

"After all," Judge Bayton said, "this is all on *voir dire*, and defense counsel apparently has some plan in view, but the Court doesn't care to have its time taken up with opinions and conclusions regardless of whether there are objections. Let's get along with the case."

"Did this evidence cause you to make a further search of the premises in the vicinity of the place where this piece of cloth was found?"

Tragg hesitated a moment, then said, "Well, yes."

"And if it hadn't been for that piece of cloth there on the

116

fence, it is quite probable that you wouldn't have searched the surrounding country?''

Tragg permitted himself a frosty smile. "Anything is possible, Mr. Mason.''

"And did your search of the surrounding country disclose other evidence which *did* substantiate the defendant's story?''

"There were tracks,'' Lt. Tragg said, "but these tracks were all a part of fabricated evidence.''

"How do you know?''

"The ground was in two general classifications, or perhaps I should say three. First, there was the surface of the road. This was a dirt road which had been rained on and which showed tracks which could have been followed on the night of the fifth, but which were pretty well obliterated by the rain which came afterward, and which definitely were not visible on the sixth or the seventh. The second class of soil was the soft soil on the side of the road. There were depressions on the side of the road in which surplus water from the road had drained. That soil remained soft for some time. The same was true of the bank leading down to the westerly side of the road. On the other side of the fence, on the west of the road, we came to a third classification of soil. This was soil covered with grass and other vegetation, and the ordinary footprint would have been invisible here. However, marks made by high heels were visible here and there. We did find some marks made by high heels but there was not enough of a pattern to enable us to make an accurate interpretation of the tracks, but we knew the whole evidence had been fabricated because the closest heel prints on the other side of the fence were found twenty-seven feet from the place where the piece of cloth was found.''

"These tracks would have gone unnoticed if it hadn't been for the cloth on the fence?''

"As to that I can't say.''

Mason turned to the deputy district attorney. "Do you wish to introduce this garment in evidence?''

Carson said, "I want the garment introduced in evidence.''

"Then I am going to insist that the cleaning mark be

117

traced," Mason said. "There is no evidence of ownership other than that the skirt was found in the defendant's apartment. Any evidence of ownership so far is a mere conclusion of the witness."

"There is plenty of circumstantial evidence of ownership," Carson said. "It was found in the defendant's apartment. It is her size. It was used in a hurried and futile attempt to substantiate a fabricated story."

Judge Bayton said, "Under the circumstances, the garment will be marked for identification only at this time. We will wait to admit it until the ownership has been proven. That concludes Mr. Mason's *voir dire* examination and you may continue with your direct examination of this witness, Mr. Prosecutor."

Carson turned to Tragg. "Did you find any physical evidence which negated the defendant's story?"

"Lots of it," Lt. Tragg said dryly.

"Will you please tell the Court what it was?"

"In the first place, the shoes worn by the decedent had not been worn on a muddy road. They were entirely free from mud. The trousers worn by the decedent had not been out in any wet brush. The clothes worn by the decedent did not have any mud on them, as would have been the case if he had slid under a barbed-wire fence. The dinner of ham and eggs which the defendant stated had not been touched had actually been eaten."

Carson turned triumphantly to Mason. "You may cross-examine."

Mason frowned thoughtfully. "You examined the shoes worn by the decedent?"

"We did."

"And found no traces of mud?"

"None whatever."

"The cuffs of the trousers?"

"No traces of mud, no indications that they had been in any wet vegetation. If the decedent had been running around through the grass on the other side of the fence, or if he had been splashing around through the mud on the road, his garments would have so indicated. There would have been un-

118

mistakable traces of soil and mud on the shoes, and the lower part of the trousers would have been soaked."

"Directing your attention to the apartment of the defendant," Mason said, "did you find underwear which was stained with mud?"

"We did."

"Did you make an attempt to find out whether that soil was the same as that in the vicinity of the Lamont lodge?"

"We did not."

"May I ask why?"

"We considered the garments a plant, just the same as the torn skirt which we found."

"It is always dangerous," Mason said, "to jump to conclusions, Lieutenant. I suggest that the police endeavor to check the stained garments with the soil at the scene of the crime, and I have no further questions."

"Are there any further questions?" Judge Bayton asked Carson.

"I have a further question of Lieutenant Tragg, in view of the situation which has developed."

"Very well, go ahead."

Carson turned to Lt. Tragg. "Did you mark for identification the shoes and trousers which the decedent was wearing?"

"I did."

"And do you have those garments with you?"

"They are available. It would take me a few moments to get them."

"Could you have them here within ten minutes?"

"I'm quite sure I could."

"May we ask the Court for a ten-minute recess," Carson asked, "in order to get these garments here?"

"Very well," Judge Bayton said. "We will take a ten-minute recess. However, it would certainly seem that the prosecution should have anticipated the necessity for introducing these garments. The Court will take this ten-minute recess, but that will be the last indulgence which will be given. If there are any other items of evidence which the

119

prosecution wishes to introduce, be sure that they are here, Mr. Prosecutor.''

Judge Bayton arose and walked into his chambers.

Mason turned to Arlene Ferris. "Look here, Arlene," he said, "I'm going to be brutally frank with you. The most expensive luxury that you can indulge in is that of lying to your lawyer."

She nodded.

"If you have lied to me," Mason went on, "you're in a mess and I don't think I can get you out. But in any event, if you *have* lied, I want to know it now."

"I've told you the absolute truth, Mr. Mason."

Mason shook his head. "If they produce those shoes and those trousers, and the shoes don't show mud stains, the bottom of the trouser legs don't show indications of having been wet, as would be the case where a person ran through wet brush, you're either going to prison for life or to the gas chamber."

"I can't help it, Mr. Mason. I've told you the absolute truth."

Mason became thoughtfully silent.

She said, "Couldn't the murderer have changed clothes on the corpse after . . ."

"Oh, sure," Mason said sarcastically, "just try selling that idea to a jury. The murderer knows that you're going to have a fight with Loring Lamont and run out on him in Lamont's own car. The murderer goes out there with an extra pair of trousers, socks and shoes. He waits until Loring Lamont comes back to the lodge, then he stabs him, then he opens the man's mouth and shoves ham and eggs down his throat, then he takes off his pants and socks and shoes and dresses the corpse—just try to stand up in front of a jury of twelve reasonably intelligent individuals and sell them an idea of that sort."

Arlene Ferris was near tears. "But that's what *must* have happened."

Mason shook his head and turned away.

Tragg returned to court carrying a bag.

Judge Bayton again came to the bench. Court was called to order, and Carson resumed his questioning.

"You now have the clothes the decedent was wearing when his body was found?"

"Yes, sir."

"I would like to have you first produce the shoes."

"Yes, sir," Tragg said, and, opening the bag, took out a pair of shoes.

"These are the shoes the decedent was wearing?"

"They are."

"What is their condition now, with reference to the condition when they were found on the body?"

"The shoes are in *exactly* the same condition except for chalk marks which have been placed upon the soles."

"What was the purpose of those chalk marks?"

"Identifying marks, so we could identify the shoes later on."

Carson walked over to the witness, took the two shoes, came back and handed them to Mason for the lawyer's inspection.

Mason turned the shoes over in his hands, carefully keeping his face without expression.

"We move that these shoes be introduced in evidence," Donald Carson said.

Mason arose. "Once more, Your Honor, I wish to examine the witness on *voir dire*."

"Very well."

Mason turned to Lt. Tragg. "Have you," he asked, "any way of knowing that these were the shoes the decedent was wearing at the time he was killed?"

"Only that they were on the feet of the corpse when I first saw it."

"Did you make any effort to search the cabin or lodge to see whether there were other garments?"

Tragg's voice showed a certain amount of indignation. "Of course we did. We searched that lodge from one end to the other, Mr. Mason."

"Did the decedent have *any* clothing there?"

"The decedent had no clothing there, no clothing of any

sort other than the following exceptions—one pair of tennis shoes, the same size as those worn by the decedent, one pair of Bermuda shorts, two short-sleeved sports jackets, two pairs of swimming trunks, one terry-cloth robe, one pair of sandals, one linen golf cap.''

"Were there other clothes there?" Mason asked.

"None that would possibly fit the decedent. The decedent's shoes were size ten and a half.''

But you did find other clothing on the premises?''

"The decedent's father, Jarvis P. Lamont, had some coveralls, cook aprons and shoes there but the shoes of Jarvis P. Lamont were eight and a half. Loring Lamont could not possibly have worn his father's clothes.''

"You examined the place thoroughly?''

"We virtually tore the place to pieces," Lt. Tragg said, "and that includes the dressing rooms at the pool.''

"The place was provisioned with liquor and food?" Mason asked.

"Well provisioned with liquor, with frozen food and canned food. There were very few perishables. There was a supply of linen for the beds, plenty of blankets, a frozen-food locker well filled with frozen food, but, for instance, there wasn't any fresh bread in the place. There was, however, a bowl in which biscuit dough had been mixed, a pan containing biscuits which had been baked in the electric oven. Six biscuits had been eaten from the pan. There were six left in the pan. There was a frying pan with grease in it, in which cooking had been done recently. The grease was ham grease. There was a smaller pan in which eggs had apparently been fried because there were bits of the cooked egg white adhering to the pan near the outer edges. There were plates from which food had been eaten . . .'' Tragg turned to Donald Carson and said, "Do you want all of this now, or am I supposed to answer only about the clothing?''

"Tell about it now if the defense has no objection," Carson said.

Lt. Tragg nodded. "Two plates which contained portions of egg yolk, particles of ham grease, a can of butter which had been opened and from which some butter had been taken, a jar of jam, small bread and butter plates on which there were biscuit crumbs and remnants of jam. There were cups and saucers.''

"How many cups and saucers?" Mason asked.

"Two. These contained small amounts of coffee. There was a percolator with coffee in it, and there were two water glasses. The dirty dishes were found on a table in the dining room, the pans and cooking utensils on the stove in the kitchen.''

"I have no further questions at this time," Mason said.

You mean that concludes your *voir dire* examination?" Judge Bayton asked.

"Yes, Your Honor. I have no further questions at this time on the *voir dire* examination in regard to the shoes. This does not mean that I waive my right to cross-examine the witness about these articles, nor do I waive my right to question the witness on *voir dire* regarding any other garments which may be produced.''

"Very well," Judge Bayton said. "The prosecutor will proceed.''

Carson said, "Now what about the trousers, Lieutenant?''

Lt. Tragg produced a pair of neatly creased trousers.

"These were the ones the decedent was wearing when the body was found?" Carson asked.

"Yes.''

"I call your attention to certain stains near the top of the trousers and ask you if you know what those stains are.''

"Yes, sir. They're bloodstains.''

"They were on the trousers when the body was found?''

"Yes, sir.''

"And the trousers were on the body?''

"Yes, sir.''

"I offer these trousers in evidence," Carson said, "together with the shoes as People's appropriate exhibits.''

"No objections," Mason said.

"Do you have any *voir dire* examination on the trousers?" Judge Bayton asked.

"None, Your Honor.''

"I think that concludes my examination of Lieutenant Tragg," Carson said.

"Cross-examination?" Judge Bayton asked.

"You said that you searched the place thoroughly. Is that correct, Lieutenant?" Mason asked.

"We searched the place thoroughly," Tragg said. "We all but tore it apart."

"You looked in the writing desk?"

"We looked in the writing desk."

"Did you find some papers in there?"

"We did."

"Did you find a checkbook on the California Second National?"

"We did."

"With check stubs?"

"Yes, sir."

"Do you know whose checkbook that was?"

"We know that the writing on some of the check stubs was that of Loring Lamont and the checks which matched those stubs had been cashed and they were signed by Loring Lamont."

"All of the checks?"

"One of them was missing."

"What one was that?"

"A stub which purported to show that a five-hundred-dollar check had been issued."

"To whom was that check issued?"

"To no one."

"What do you mean by that?"

"The check had evidently been made out and for some reason had been torn from the checkbook *after* the amount had been written on the check stub. The stub had then been marked O.K. to show that it was all right to have a check stub there for five hundred dollars without the name of the payee."

"That's a conclusion?" Mason asked.

"For what it's worth," Tragg said, "that's a conclusion. If you want the bare facts I will state that there was a check stub in the book showing the amount of five hundred dollars. The stub had nothing else on it except the letters O.K.''

"And were those letters in the handwriting of Loring Lamont?''

"I don't know.''

"The check, of which this was the stub, had been torn off on the day of the murder?''

"I don't know that.''

"You don't?'' Mason asked.

"No.''

"There was another check stub immediately in front of that check stub payable to Orval Kingman, was there not?''

"That's right.''

"And this other check would naturally have been torn off after that first check?''

"I object on the ground that the question is argumentative and calls for a conclusion of the witness,'' Carson said.

Judge Bayton nodded his head.

"Just a moment,'' Carson said suddenly. "I will withdraw the objection. I'd like to have Lieutenant Tragg answer that question.''

"The question is argumentative and calls for a conclusion of the witness,'' Judge Bayton pointed out wearily. "The Court doesn't need the opinions of witnesses. The Court wants facts.''

"Nevertheless, Your Honor, I would like to have Lieutenant Tragg give the answer so that we can have it in the record.''

"Well, if you withdraw the objection I'll let the witness answer this one question,'' Judge Bayton said, "but I don't want to take up time having a lot of argumentative questions even if they aren't objected to. You may answer this one question, Lieutenant.''

"The answer,'' Lt. Tragg said, "is that in my opinion, for what it is worth, Loring Lamont started to make Orval Kingman a check for five hundred dollars on the wrong check. Then, realizing his mistake, he tore off that check and destroyed it, marked O.K. on the stub to show that it was all right to have a blank stub at that point and then made the

125

check to Orval Kingman on the check which he should have used."

Mason smiled. "It is your opinion then that this was done inadvertently and that Loring Lamont, running through the check stubs, inadvertently turned over a check stub to which the check itself was attached without noticing what he was doing?"

"I think he must have," Tragg said.

"That's rather unlikely, isn't it?" Mason asked. "A man running through check stubs would certainly know when he came to a stub to which the check was attached."

"That's what I think happened," Lt. Tragg said.

"You didn't impound this checkbook as evidence?"

"Evidence of what?"

"Evidence of the activities of the decedent on the last day of his life."

"We did not. We made a list of the checks and that's all."

"Where is this checkbook now?"

"As far as I know it's still in the desk. I will state that Sadie Richmond telephoned me that you had instructed her to turn the checkbook over to the police but . . ."

"Now just a moment," Judge Bayton interrupted, "this inquiry is going altogether too far afield. We're now getting hearsay evidence. If the defense wishes, it certainly is entitled to bring that checkbook into court. However, I don't know what bearing it could have on the case."

"If the Court please," Mason said, "it indicates that Loring Lamont had the checkbook with him when he went to the lodge. It indicates that he took the checkbook out of his pocket and, in my opinion, made a check for five hundred dollars to someone whose initials were O.K. That he was in a hurry and so simply put the initials of the payee on the stub."

"Was the stub dated?" Judge Bayton asked.

"It was not. Just the figure five hundred dollars and the initials were on it."

"But what if your assumption is correct?" Judge Bayton asked. "What would you expect to prove by that?"

126

"It would prove that someone else had been out at that lodge that evening."

"You may introduce the checkbook in evidence as part of your case if you want to," Judge Bayton said, "but I can assure you, Mr. Mason, it would take more persuasive evidence than that for the Court to feel that someone else had been out there. Do you have any further questions on cross-examination?"

"No further questions," Mason said.

"Very well," Judge Bayton said to Lt. Tragg. "You may stand down."

"If the Court please," Carson said, "the People have no further witnesses we care to call, at least at this time. We may have rebuttal evidence."

Mason was on his feet. "Just a moment," he said. "We have a right to cross-examine Peter Lyons."

"Oh, yes," Carson said. "I have sent for Lyons. Just a moment. I will call him."

Carson turned to an officer who sat beside him and engaged in a whispered conversation.

Abruptly the deputy district attorney frowned and became vehement. The officer shook his head.

Carson bent closer. There was a whispered conference again, then Carson straightened and said, "Your Honor, a most embarrassing situation has developed. It seems that this is Peter Lyons' day off. He is out somewhere and can't be reached. I am afraid that perhaps I am partially to blame in the matter. I told Lyons that I would need him as a witness unless the defense was willing to stipulate as to his testimony. I told him further that if the defense would stipulate as to his testimony, he would not be needed. When Mr. Mason made his stipulation I so advised my office. Someone in my office advised Mr. Lyons that there had been a stipulation as to his testimony. I am afraid there was a misunderstanding all around. In fact, I am free to confess to the Court that I, myself, did not appreciate the full technical significance of Mr. Mason's stipulation until he raised the point that he was entitled to cross-examine the officer.

"Under the circumstances, if Mr. Mason will state the

points he expects to bring out on cross-examination, I may be able to stipulate that under cross-examination Peter Lyons would so testify."

Mason shook his head. "I want the privilege of cross-examining this witness," he said. "That was the understanding."

Judge Bayton frowned with annoyance. "Surely, Mr. Mason, you must know the type of cross-examination you expect to make and the points you expect to bring out on cross-examination."

"Frankly, Your Honor, I am at the moment working on a theory of the case that I do not care to disclose until after I first have asked certain questions of the witness—after all, this witness is a police officer, he is a witness for the prosecution, and I fail to see why I should be required to tell the deputy district attorney my entire plan of attack on cross-examination."

"Do you question his testimony?" Judge Bayton asked.

"I may question his testimony and his credibility," Mason said.

"But that is absurd!" Carson protested. "This man is a police officer. At the time he tagged the car of Loring Lamont for illegal parking he had absolutely no idea that he was doing anything other than performing a routine act. The tag which he issued was a so-called non-fixable tag, and the records are there. They speak for themselves. I have talked with Peter Lyons personally and at some length. All Peter Lyons knows about the situation is what is disclosed by the records. At the time, the Loring Lamont car was simply another car parked in front of a fireplug. He sees hundreds of them every month."

Judge Bayton glanced inquiringly at Perry Mason.

"I still want to cross-examine this witness," Mason said doggedly.

"Well," Judge Bayton said irritably, "the law gives you the right to be confronted with witnesses and to cross-examine them. If you insist upon that right, I suppose the Court has no alternative except to continue the case until tomorrow morning at ten o'clock. However, I wish to point

128

out to both counsel that there is a backlog of cases, that under instructions from the Judicial Council we are trying to get caught up, that in the opinion of the Court this case shouldn't have taken more than half a day. It was continued into the afternoon, and now apparently the Court will be forced to waste a large part of the afternoon and again resume the case tomorrow morning."

"I'm sorry," Mason said. "The mistake wasn't mine. I specifically stated in my stipulation that I would stipulate if Lyons would so testify on direct examination."

"The prosecutor should have noticed the obligation which was placed upon him to have the witness available for cross-examination," Judge Bayton snapped. "Court will adjourn until ten o'clock tomorrow morning. The defendant is remanded to the custody of the sheriff. I will point out, however, to defense counsel that unless there is some cross-examination of the officer, Peter Lyons, which indicates that the defense has some pertinent theory which it is following up, the Court will feel that it has been imposed upon.

"That is all. Court is adjourned until ten o'clock tomorrow morning."

Mason turned to Arlene Ferris. "Have you," he asked, "anything else to tell me?"

She was almost in tears as she shook her head in tight-lipped negation.

"Very well," Mason said. "I'll see you tomorrow morning."

Chapter 12

Mason sat at his office desk, drumming silently with his finger tips on the blotter. In an ash tray by his right hand, a neglected cigarette was slowly being consumed to ash, a wisp of smoke moving steadily upward in a straight line, then turning into a spiral before dispersing in little wisps of faint-blue smoke.

Della Street, knowing his moods, sat on the other side of the desk, pencil poised over a shorthand book, remaining absolutely motionless so that she would not interfere with his concentration.

Mason, his eyes level-lidded with thought, said at length, "Take this down, Della. Let us start out with the supposition that Arlene has lied to us. The physical evidence is directly opposed to her story. Why did she lie? Dash-dash. Was it because she's guilty? Dash-dash. If that is the case, she would have made up a lie that would have fitted the facts. That girl is reasonably intelligent. Why does she tell a lie which doesn't fit the facts?"

Della Street completed taking down Mason's comments, then waited.

After a few minutes, Mason said, "She must be protecting someone. But how would such a story protect anyone, and who is that someone? Dash-dash. Who could it be?"

Slowly, almost imperceptibly, Mason shook his head.

He pushed back his chair from the desk, ground out the cigarette in the ash tray, got up and started pacing the floor.

Suddenly Mason stopped mid-stride, whirled, said to Della Street, "All right, Della, take this. Suppose client is not lying? Dash-dash. Then why don't the physical facts agree with her story? Dash-dash. The only possible solution is, we have an incomplete story."

130

Mason smacked his fist against the desk. "Hang it, Della," he exclaimed, "make a note! I want a sign made and I want it hung on the wall just back of my desk. *Try to have confidence in your clients.*"

"You think she's telling the truth?" Della Street asked.

"She's telling the truth," Mason said, "and I have fallen into the worst trap a defense attorney can ever fall into."

"What's that?" Della Street asked apprehensively.

"Letting myself get hypnotized by the reasoning of the prosecution and thinking that things happened the way the prosecution says they happened just because evidence seems to support them."

Della Street, knowing that in moments like this, Mason wanted someone to help him clarify his thinking, said, "You mean the evidence is open to two interpretations."

"It has to be," Mason said. "The key witness is Peter Lyons, that police officer they were so reluctant to produce."

"You feel they were reluctant?" she asked.

"Of course they were," Mason said. "They tried every way in the world to keep me from cross-examining Peter Lyons. Now, what the devil does Peter Lyons have to say that is going to upset their applecart?"

"They make him sound like a very unimportant witness," Della Street said.

"That's the point," Mason said. "They're deliberately playing him down because they're afraid I'm going to play him up. Now why?"

"What reason *could* there be?" Della Street asked.

"Because," Mason said, "Peter Lyons is going to testify to something that will help my case. They've tried their damnedest to keep me from cross-examining him. This business of Lyons being where he can't be located is sheer nonsense. It's a stall."

"Why?" Della Street asked.

"Let's analyze why," Mason said. "A lawyer always has to look at things logically and from an independent viewpoint. Any time he gets off on the wrong track because of taking something for granted, he's lost. Now then, we know

131

what Peter Lyons is going to testify to because Donald Carson told us."

"But did the deputy district attorney state the truth?" Della Street asked .

"Sure, he did," Mason said. "He wouldn't dare do otherwise. He would be guilty of unprofessional conduct of misleading the Court, of prejudicial misconduct in the case . . . no, he *had* to tell the truth. But he didn't have to tell *all* the truth.

"Now, as I remember the statement made by the deputy district attorney, Peter Lyons would testify that he found Loring Lamont's car in front of a fireplug at nine o'clock, that he gave a citation for illegal parking which presumably he would have tied on the steering wheel of the car—now, why don't they want me to cross-examine him about that?"

Della Street shook her head in puzzled contemplation, while Mason once more resumed pacing the floor.

"Arlene Ferris tells me she left the car in front of the fireplug, so Peter Lyons' testimony would agree with hers. Now then, remember that Peter Lyons only gave one citation. He . . ."

Mason stopped abruptly, turned to face Della Street, said in a low voice, "Well, I'll be damned!"

"What's the matter?" Della Street asked.

"The matter is," Mason said, "I've been unspeakably naïve. I've been a babe in the woods. Of course, they don't want me to cross-examine Peter Lyons! Peter Lyons is going to testify to something that will be diametrically opposed to the facts as they understand them, and . . . that's it! That has to be it!"

"What?" Della Street asked.

"Peter Lyons is going to testify that he came back later on before he went off duty, some time between nine o'clock and midnight, *and the car was gone.*"

"Gone?" Della Street asked. "How could it have been gone? It was there in front of the fireplug all night."

"It was gone," Mason said, "because Arlene Ferris left the keys in the ignition. Somebody came along, took that car away and then brought it back and parked it again right in

132

front of the fireplug so the other two officers who came on duty at midnight found the car there and proceeded to issue citations for parking violations, and then, toward morning, had the car towed away.''

"But why should anyone take it and then bring it back?'' Della Street asked.

"That,'' Mason said, "is what we're going to find out, and we're going to begin looking in the place where we should have looked right at the start.''

"Where?''

"We're going to talk with Edith Bristol, private secretary of J. P. Lamont, and George Albert, the office manager.''

"How come?'' Della Street asked.

"We're going to get the evidence in order this time,'' Mason said. "Remember what Arlene Ferris told us. There were lots of people wanting to go to work for the Lamont Company. The company had a waiting list of persons applying for secretarial positions, but Arlene Ferris simply told Madge Elwood she wanted a job. Madge Elwood spoke to somebody and immediately and forthwith Arlene Ferris was given a job. George Albert said that Loring Lamont issued some sort of an executive order just before he left for South America. Thereafter the whole personnel department was brushed aside and Arlene was put to work.''

Della Street's eyes widened. "That's right, Chief!''

"And the devil of it is,'' Mason said angrily, "the whole evidence was right there in front of me all the time and I damn near muffed it. Come on, Della, let's go.''

"Just what are we after?'' Della Street asked.

"The truth,'' Mason told her.

They hurried down to the parking lot, got Mason's car and drove to the executive offices of the Lamont Company.

Mason told the receptionist, "I want to see Edith Bristol, J. P. Lamont's secretary, and I also want to see George Albert, the office manager. I'm Perry Mason, the attorney, and it's important.''

"Just a minute,'' the receptionist said.

She put through a telephone call, said, "Very well, hold on,'' and turned to Perry Mason. "Miss Bristol says that she doesn't think the district attorney would want her to talk with you.''

Mason said grimly, "All right, then I'll subpoena her as a witness and I'll show bias by showing that she wouldn't talk with anyone because she was afraid she'd hurt the district attorney's feelings.''

"Just a minute," the receptionist said, and again turned to the telephone, talking rapidly.

After a few moments she said, "Very well. She'll see you. Take the elevator to the third floor. Miss Bristol will be waiting at the elevator for you."

Mason and Della Street entered the elevator. At the third floor, as the elevator door opened, a young woman stepped forward. "I'm Edith Bristol," she said. "Will you come to my office, please?''

She led the way down a corridor, past stenographers who were clacking away at typewriters and who looked up with surreptitious curiosity as the trio walked past.

In the office Edith Bristol closed the door, indicated seats and said, "Just what is it you want, Mr. Mason?''

Mason surveyed her in thoughtful appraisal. "I had hardly expected one so young in so important a position," he said.

"What is it you want, please?" she asked once more, her tone cold with formality.

Mason said, "I want to know just why it was that Arlene Ferris asked her friend, Madge Elwood, to get her a job here, and within a couple of days Arlene Ferris was at work, apparently by some order that was issued directly from Loring Lamont.''

Edith Bristol lowered her eyes. "I'm sure I couldn't tell you," she said. "You said you wanted to see the office manager."

Mason nodded.

"Perhaps he can tell you."

"He was on the witness stand," Mason said, "and he didn't seem to have any idea except that she had been put to work on the direct orders of Loring Lamont. I think someone else can tell me why Loring Lamont took the trouble to intervene. Can you tell me that?''

She slowly shook her head. "I am afraid there's not very much I can tell you, Mr. Mason. I know that occasionally persons were employed because of certain personal contacts. Miss Elwood, I believe, worked here for some two years and her work was very highly thought of. Did you intend to ask the office manager?"

"I did," Mason said.

"Perhaps we'd better get him in here."

Edith Bristol picked up a telephone and said, "Connect me with George Albert, please."

After a moment, she said, "Mr. Albert, Mr. Perry Mason, the attorney, is here in the office. He is accompanied by Miss Della Street, his secretary, who is apparently prepared to take notes. Mr. Mason wants to know how it happened that Arlene Ferris was employed without going through the usual channels in the personnel department, and wants to know how it happened that Madge Elwood was able to bring to bear enough influence to have Miss Ferris put on ahead of the waiting list. Would you mind coming to my office and answering Mr. Mason's question? Yes, right away, please."

She hung up the phone, smiled at Mason and said, "Perhaps we can get the matter clarified, Mr. Mason. I'm quite certain that no directive came through his office. In other words, Mr. Jarvis P. Lamont knew nothing about it; therefore, I know nothing about it. You will understand that Mr. Lamont, Senior, had not been in the office since he learned of his son's murder. However, I have been his secretary for some two years and I can assure you that any preferential treatment given Miss Ferris was not because of any directive issued by him."

Mason, frowning thoughtfully, nodded. His manner was completely preoccupied.

They sat silently for a few moments, waiting for George Albert. Mason stirred uneasily, looked toward the door, then back at Edith Bristol.

"I'd like to know a little about how Loring Lamont lived," he said. "He didn't live with his father?"

"No."

"He had an apartment of his own?"

"Yes."

"That was at 9612 Endicott Way?"

"Yes."

"He had perhaps a cook, a housekeeper, a Filipino boy?"

"No."

"Then he must have eaten out a good deal of the time."

"I wouldn't know."

"He took an active part in the business here?"

"Yes."

"Did he have any particular position in the firm?"

"Vice president."

"He traveled quite a bit?"

"Yes."

"And, I take it, he and his father were fond of each other?"

"Yes."

Mason smiled. "You don't seem to volunteer much in the way of information."

"I'm not being paid to volunteer information, Mr. Mason. I don't even know whether Mr. Jarvis P. Lamont is going to approve of this meeting."

The door of the office was pushed open. George Albert entered the room, smiled a greeting at Perry Mason, then glanced quickly at Edith Bristol.

"You know Mr. Albert," Edith Bristol said.

"I've met him in court," Perry Mason said. "This is Della Street, my secretary. I want to get some information about Arlene Ferris and how she got her job."

"I'm afraid I can't tell you very much more than I told you on the witness stand."

"I think you can," Mason said. "It certainly wasn't the custom for Loring Lamont to intercede personally in connection with jobs in the business. There was a personnel department, and I take it the hiring was in the hands of the personnel department."

"Yes."

"Yet in the case of Arlene Ferris, Loring Lamont issued a directive."

"That's right."

"Now then," Mason said, "it seems that Arlene Ferris

136

went to her friend, Madge Elwood, that Madge had worked here at one time and Madge was the point of contact."

"That could well be," Albert said.

"What do you mean by that?"

"I mean that Miss Elwood could very well have telephoned Loring Lamont and asked him to put Arlene Ferris on the payroll."

"And Loring Lamont would have done it?"

"He did it, didn't he?"

"Do you know that Madge Elwood telephoned him?"

"I don't *know* it, no. I'm only drawing conclusions from what you yourself have said. After all, you're Arlene Ferris' attorney. She must have told you how she got the job."

"Perhaps she doesn't know," Mason said.

Albert shrugged his shoulders.

"Yet," Mason said, "knowing that Arlene Ferris was, so to speak, under the protection of one of the big executives of the company, you had no hesitancy about firing her."

"I try to keep efficiency in the office, Mr. Mason. That's my job. I can't let some young woman indulge in impudence simply because she may be friendly with one of the Lamonts. They don't pay me to run an office that way."

"When did you first know Arlene Ferris was coming to work?"

"Loring Lamont told me."

"What did he say?"

"He handed me a folded slip of paper. That was before he left for South America. The name Arlene Ferris was on it. He said, 'Put her to work as an expert stenographer at the top salary we pay.' "

"So Arlene went to work without any test, as far as you know, and started drawing top pay right at the start?"

"I believe those are the facts."

"And you don't know any more about the situation than that?"

"That's all."

"Had that ever happened before with anyone else?" Mason asked. "In other words, had anyone else ever been put to work in exactly that way?"

"The applications are regularly channeled through personnel."

"I'm not asking about regular applications. I'm asking if this particular thing had ever happened before."

Albert said, "I would have to consult the records, and . . ."

"Quit hedging," Mason said. "I'm going to call you back to the witness stand if I have to. Now, there's something funny going on here."

"What do you mean?" Albert asked, drawing himself up belligerently.

"You know what I mean," Mason said. "You're stalling around. You're covering up, both of you. When Miss Bristol asked you to come in here, she didn't pick up the phone and say to the operator, 'Ask George Albert to come in here.' Instead, she asked for you personally on the phone, then when she got you she didn't say, 'Can you come into my office for a minute,' but she went on to tell you all about Mr. Perry Mason, the attorney, being in the office, all about what I wanted, all about my secretary being with me. Even then you didn't come in here right away. You stopped to think things over and have the answers ready.

"Now let's quit stalling around on this thing. How many other people came to work in this office because of directives of Loring Lamont?"

"I only know of one," Albert said.

"Who?"

"Madge Elwood."

"George!" Edith Bristol exclaimed, her voice a whiplash of sharp rebuke.

"I can't help it," Albert said. "What's the use of stalling? You haven't seem him in court. I have. He'd do exactly what he said. He'd get me in court and bring it out on the witness stand."

"What I want to know," Mason said, turning to Edith Bristol, "is why *you* were trying to keep *that* under cover."

Edith Bristol said coldly, "I think, Mr. Mason, we are going to terminate this interview. You now have the information you want. I may state that you have all the information we can give you."

138

"All right," Mason said, "if you want to put it that way, we'll put it that way."

He whipped two documents from his pocket, handed one to Edith Bristol, one to George Albert.

"What are these?" Edith Bristol asked.

"Subpoenas to appear in court at ten o'clock tomorrow morning in the case of the People versus Arlene Ferris and testify on behalf of the defendant as defense witnesses," Mason said.

"I'll expect to see you there. I'll resume my interrogations at that time. Good afternoon."

Mason and Della Street left the office.

"Now what?" Della Street asked.

"First we telephone Paul Drake and see what he's learned," Mason said. "There's a telephone booth there on the sidewalk."

Della Street put through the call, got Paul Drake on the line, then motioned excitedly to Perry Mason.

"Paul has something on Otto Keswick," she said. "He's checked on Keswick's alibi."

She extended the receiver to Mason, who entered the telephone booth. "Hello, Paul. What is it?" Mason asked.

"A couple of things," Drake said. "I checked up with Mrs. Arthur Sparks, who has the house where Otto Keswick rooms. Keswick was correct in saying he does odd jobs around the place in order to earn his room rent.

"On the night of the fifth they were watching television all right, but Mrs. Sparks wasn't with him after seven-thirty. She sat and watched television with him until then. But she had a splitting headache and went to bed. She says that Keswick *could* have gone out, although she doesn't think so. She knows that he kept the television on because she couldn't get into a really sound sleep. She would doze off for a while, then snap wide awake. She heard the television every time she wakened. Finally it was turned off at ten-thirty, because she remembers the program finishing. But that doesn't mean that she can testify Keswick was there between seven-thirty and ten-thirty."

"I see," Mason said thoughtfully.

139

"Now then," Drake went on, "here's something else. A fellow who has the adjoining piece of property on the north has a nice little cabin on the property. He works as a bookkeeper and Lamonts don't consider him in their social class at all. In other words, they aren't neighborly. He may have a slight resentment on account of that. It's hard to tell. Anyway, he had cut a road on the south side of this property. That side adjoins the Lamont property on the north. Last year some storm water ran down this new road and washed a ditch. That ditch had thrown water on the Lamont property and they threatened to sue him.

"On the night of the fifth, knowing that it had started to rain, this fellow was a little concerned about whether the embankments he had thrown up would keep the water out of the road and off the Lamont property. He went out just to make certain. He says that shortly after he turned into his property and had switched out the lights on his car, another car came along the road and went through the gate at the Lamont property. Now, *he* says that the gate was open—that the car drove slowly through and came to a stop, that he knows the car driven by Otto Keswick, that it has a peculiar piston slap, and he's positive this was Keswick's car. He says he heard voices, and he thinks he heard the voice of Sadie Richmond, but he can't swear it."

"What's his name?" Mason asked.

"George Banning."

"Now, that's terribly important," Mason said. "I want to talk with Banning and I want to have him subpoenaed as a witness for the defense. I want him in court tomorrow morning."

"I've already served a subpoena on him," Drake said, "and I've made arrangements for him to attend. I've fixed it up so he doesn't feel sore at all, but is going to testify to what he knows. I think he's a little bit peeved at the Lamonts."

"How long did this car stay on the place?" Mason asked.

"He doesn't know. Banning just looked around enough to make sure that his new drainage system was keeping the water out of the road and sending it on down to the east, so that it would miss the Lamont property entirely. The water

140

had already begun to wash a channel. He stayed only long enough to check on that and then drove back to the city.

"He says lights were on in the Lamont lodge the entire time he was there, and that lights were on when he left. He also says the gate must have been open, because the car didn't stop at the gate, and he knows that an automobile was in there when he drove out."

"What time was it?" Mason asked.

"He can't fix the time exactly. It was right around seven-thirty to seven-forty-five."

Mason said, "Okay, Paul, I think we've hit pay dirt. That indicates Otto Keswick was lying. That last check for five hundred dollars must have been made to Keswick. I think he failed to present it at the bank because he knew Loring Lamont was dead and therefore the check was valueless."

"And why did Lamont do such a hurried job on the check stub?"

"Because," Mason said, "he . . . damn it, Paul, there's only one reason for him to do such a hurried job on that check stub and that's because he *was* in a hurry."

"I'll keep digging," Drake said.

"Do that," Mason told him. "Now, here's something else, Paul. I told Madge Elwood to be in court this afternoon. She didn't show up. I'm going to run down to Santa Monica and see if I can contact her at her apartment, but I wish you'd start looking around a bit and see if you can pick her up."

"And if I do?" Drake asked.

"Throw a tail on her."

"Okay, will do," Drake said, and hung up.

Chapter 13

Mason and Della Street drove in silence until they reached the Kelsington Apartments.

Mason rang Madge Elwood's apartment repeatedly, got no answer. He then went to the manager. She was a middle-aged, capable-looking woman. "I'm trying to get in touch with Madge Elwood," he said. "It's very important. She doesn't seem to be in, but I would like to check and make certain."

"I don't think she's in," the manager said. "I saw her leaving this afternoon. She had two suitcases. Apparently she's going someplace and intending to be away for some time. Have you inquired at the place where she works?"

"Do you know the place where she works?" Mason asked.

"No. She has a secretarial job here somewhere with an advertising firm—anyway, they'd be closed now. I'm sorry I can't give you any help."

"Would it be possible for you to use your passkey and just take a quick look in the apartment to see if she's . . ."

The manager shook her head. "I'm sorry. We don't pry into the affairs of tenants. They pay their rent. They come and they go as they please. We try not to take an undue interest in what they do, and we are very careful not to give out information. I may have told you too much already, but— I recognized you, of course, from your photographs and I know you're interested in a case in which Miss Elwood is involved in some way, so I thought it would be all right to tell you that she took two suitcases and left."

"Thanks a lot," Mason said. "Do you know whether she drove off in her car or whether she took a taxicab?"

"I'm sure I couldn't tell you that. I just happened to see her coming out of the elevator with these two suitcases. They were too heavy for her to carry both at once, so she took them out one at a time. I guess that must mean she went somewhere in her own car. If she had gone in a cab, the cabdriver would have picked up one of the suitcases.''

Mason said, "Do me one more favor. Does she pay her rent by check or with cash?''

"By check.''

"And do you remember the bank?''

She said, "There's no reason why I shouldn't tell you that, I guess. Her account is in the neighborhood bank right around the corner. It caters to office workers and stays open until seven-thirty every night except Saturday.''

"You say it's around the corner?''

"Go to the right as you leave the apartment, turn right again at the first corner and it's midway in the block.''

"Thanks a lot,'' Mason said.

He and Della Street left the apartment and went to the bank.

"I want to talk with the manager,'' Perry Mason said.

"It's a matter of some importance. My name is Perry Mason, I'm a lawyer, and . . .''

"Oh, yes. Just a minute. If you'll step right this way, please, and wait for just a few minutes.''

Mason followed the young woman into an office, waited some two minutes and was then introduced to the manager of the bank as he came bustling in.

"What can I do for you, Mr. Mason?'' the manager asked.

Mason said, "This is perhaps a little irregular, but I can assure you that it's highly important. I want to know something about the status of Madge Elwood's account.''

The manager shook his head. "I'm sorry. We can't give out any information of that sort.''

Mason said, "I'm very much concerned because I have reason to believe she cashed a check this afternoon and I think the check may have been a forgery.''

"Well, of course, *that's* different,'' the manager said. "We're always interested in detecting forgeries.''

"If you'll consult your records,'' Mason said. "I think you'll find that the check she cashed this afternoon is worthless. I'd like to get in touch with her before she draws on the account.''

"Just a moment," the manager said, his voice showing great concern. "You wait right here, Mr. Mason.''

When the manager had left, Della Street glanced quizzically at the lawyer. "What makes you think she cashed a check this afternoon?"

"If she's going someplace she needs cash," Mason said.

"Then why wouldn't she simply make a withdrawal from her account?"

"She would. In that case, the bank manager will let us know, either by telling us so, or else by inadvertently letting the cat out of the bag. He'll come back and say, 'You're mistaken, Mr. Mason. The only check which went through her account this afternoon was her own check.' ''

Della Street nodded.

"On the other hand," Mason said, "if someone has financed her flight, there's just a chance we'll find out who that someone is.''

Della Street thought the situation over and smiled. "It's what you call a daring approach and a direct approach.''

"Those approaches sometimes pay off," Mason said. "Bear in mind that in this case we're dealing with a branch bank that caters to payroll deposits. It probably has very few large transactions and the manager would be particularly embarrassed if he sustained any loss through a forgery. He . . .''

Mason broke off abruptly as the manager, looking very disturbed, re-entered the office.

"Mr. Mason," he said, "this is highly unusual and highly irregular. Can you tell me what makes you believe that the check was forged?"

"Frankly, I cannot," Mason said. "I have reason to believe, however, that she, in all innocence, may have cashed a check which was a forgery. If there was such a transaction, I suggest you take steps to verify the check.''

The manager said, "Just a minute." He once more left the office, then came back and seated himself at the desk. His face was very plainly worried.

After a moment, the phone rang.

144

The manager picked up the phone, gave his name and position, said, "I am inquiring about a check which was cashed this afternoon by Madge Elwood. The transaction is a little out of the ordinary. The check is rather large and I would like to verify it. Is it possible for me to reach Mr. Jarvis P. Lamont?"

The banker was silent, listening for a few minutes, then abruptly the look of worry left his face. "Well, thank you very much," he said. "I was just checking, that's all . . . no, thank you . . . no, not at all. You see, we're rather a small branch bank here and the transaction was unusual . . . yes, thank you very much. I'm sorry I bothered you, Goodby."

He hung up the phone and smiled at Mason. "No, Mr. Mason," he said, "the check was quite all right, so there's nothing for either of us to worry about."

Mason let his face break into a big smile of relief. "Well," he said, "that's something! I'm very glad to learn that. I . . ."

"Could you tell me what caused you to believe the check might be forged?" the banker asked.

"I'm sorry," Mason asked. "It evidently was a misunderstanding all around. You know how annoying these anonymous tips can be. I'm sure you must have had experience with them."

"I understand," the banker said. "It's quite all right. I talked with the personal secretary of the man who signed the check and it's good as gold. She knows all about it."

"Thanks a lot," Mason said, shaking hands. "I'm sorry I bothered you, and, under the circumstances, I'd appreciate it if you didn't mention this to anyone."

"Indeed I won't," the banker said. "We keep all of our transactions entirely confidential. Good afternoon, Mr. Mason."

The banker escorted them to the door of his office.

Outside in the street, Della Street and Perry Mason exchanged glances.

"Well," Mason said, as he walked back to the place where he had parked his car, "the plot begins to thicken."

145

"I'll say it thickens," Della Street said. "That double-crossing Edith Bristol! She knew all along about that check and . . . but why was it given?"

"The answer to that is obvious," Mason said. "The check was given to Madge Elwood because Jarvis P. Lamont wanted her out of town—so now we ask ourselves why he wanted her out of town. And the answer is that, in all probability, he was afraid I was going to put her on the witness stand.

"So now we have a beautiful puzzle, Della. Let's try to reason it out."

"Where do we begin?" Della Street asked.

"We start where we should have started in the first place," Mason said, "with Loring Lamont."

Della Street regarded him with a puzzled expression. "I don't get it."

"In order to know what happened, we have to find out what forces were at work. Now, let's for the moment assume that Arlene Ferris is telling the truth. Now, what would have happened after she left?"

"What do you mean?"

"What would Loring Lamont have done?"

"If she is telling the truth," Della Street said thoughtfully, "there is only one thing he could have done. He turned around and walked back to the rustic lodge. He went in and ate the ham and eggs, and . . ."

"Two plates?" Mason asked.

"Well," Della Street said, "he could have thrown one down the garbage disposal."

"Exactly," Mason said. "Why not two? He was hardly in a mood for cold ham and eggs. But he was in the mood for a number of other things."

Della Street nodded. "Go on."

"He wanted a drink, he wanted dry clothes, he wanted feminine companionship, and, naturally, he wanted transportation back to town."

"So he called someone who could give him the things he wanted?"

Mason nodded.

146

"Who?" she asked.

"Take a guess," Mason said.

She shook her head.

"There was only one person it could have been," Mason said. "The facts are plain as day."

"Who?"

"Madge Elwood."

Della Street looked at him, started to say something, caught herself. Slowly her eyes widened. "Then," she said, "then it was . . . it really *was* Madge Elwood that Jerome Henley saw getting out of the car?"

"Sure, it was Madge Elwood," Mason said. "Notice that Madge Elwood had pull. All she had to do was pick up the phone and say, 'I want a job for my friend, Arlene Ferris.' Immediately Loring Lamont went to George Albert and said, 'We're putting a new stenographer to work. Her name is Arlene Ferris and she's to draw top salary. She won't come to you through the personnel department. She'll come to you through me. That's all the authorization you need. Put her to work.'

"That happened in Madge Elwood's case and it happened in Arlene Ferris' case.

"So," Mason went on, "after Loring Lamont got back to the lodge he picked up the telephone and called Madge Elwood. He said, 'Madge, your friend turned out to be a nasty-tempered prude. What the devil did you mean by getting me mixed up with a girl of that sort? Now she's stolen my car and made off with it. Go to my apartment, get me some dry clothes, some shoes and get out here fast.'"

Della Street nodded, "So Madge Elwood took his car and drove out there with the dry things and . . . wait a minute, Chief. There's something wrong with that."

"What?"

"How could Madge Elwood have known his car was parked in front of his apartment? How could Loring Lamont have told her where it was?"

"Remember," Mason said, "that as soon as Arlene got back to her apartment she called Madge and told her all about how Loring Lamont had turned into a rapacious wolf and

147

that she'd taken his car, left him stranded, and had parked his car in front of a fireplug where he could pay some fines on it.''

"That's right!" Della Street exclaimed. "But isn't there a conflict in the time element?"

Mason gave the matter some thought. "Madge probably got the call from Loring Lamont, then decided to doll herself up before going to the lodge. She probably was putting on the finishing touches when she received Arlene's call."

"That would make it work out just about right," Della Street said, "but it presupposes a very intimate relationship between Madge and Loring Lamont."

"Such things have been known to happen," Mason said.

"Then that would explain a lot of things," Della Street said.

Mason nodded. "And that's why they're so anxious to keep Peter Lyons off the witness stand. He'll testify that he put a tag on the car, all right, at perhaps around nine o'clock. But he'll also testify that later on he looked for the car and didn't see it. Now, that doesn't fit in with the prosecution's theory of the case, so they don't want to bring that fact out. They're perfectly willing to state to the Court that he would testify that he found the car parked in front of a fireplug at nine o'clock and he tagged it. They want his testimony to stop right there. They don't want him stating that after that he looked for the car and couldn't find it."

"Then what happened?" Della Street asked. "Madge Elwood must have gone on out to the lodge."

"She went out there," Mason said. "She gave him his dry clothes, and then, for some reason or other, they got into quite an argument, and in the course of the argument, Madge grabbed a knife and plunged it into his back.

"Prior to that time, he had probably sought to solace his injured masculine feelings and he'd cooked up a fresh batch of ham and eggs. He and Madge Elwood had eaten the ham and eggs, and then the fight started.

"So than Madge Elwood found herself with a corpse on her hands and suddenly decided to play it smart. She knew that Arlene Ferris had been out there and had had a fight with

148

him. She knew exactly what had happened because she had the story both from Loring Lamont's lips and from Arlene's phone call. So all she had to do was to take the car back and leave it exactly where Arlene Ferris had parked it and go on back to her apartment and pretend to be innocent.

"How she must have laughed at me when I came to her and tried to get her co-operation in clearing Arlene. She was smart enough to play right into my hands, keep a poker face and keep her mouth shut."

"And Jerome Henley saw her when she was getting out of the car. But the police talked him out of that identification," Della Street said.

Mason nodded.

"And it wasn't at ten."

"Of course not," Mason said. "Everything about it indicates that it was later, but I made the mistake of not questioning the time element the way I should have because I knew that Arlene Ferris had driven the car up to the curb and parked it in front of the fireplug prior to nine o'clock—it had to be prior to nine because Peter Lyons put a tag on the car then."

"And now?" Della Street asked.

"Now," Mason said, "we're going to find Madge Elwood. We're going to force her to make a confession."

"How are we going to do that?"

"By lowering the boom on her," Mason said. "We'll show that we know exactly what happened. We'll tell her that Jerome Henley actually saw her."

"But what about Henley? Will he co-operate?"

Mason said, "He's angry and embarrassed. No man likes to have someone make a fool of him. He thought that I had made a fool of him. Police convinced him that I had rung a ringer in on him, that I had substituted Madge Elwood for Arlene Ferris, that Arlene was the girl he had actually seen. They showed him pictures, they gave him a buildup and finally convinced Henley. Actually, his first impression was the correct one. It had been Madge Elwood he had seen. He *may* be too confused now to remember anything clearly."

"Can we expect anything from him?" Della Street asked.

"I don't know," Mason said. "I can go out and put my cards on the table. I can tell him what happened and then we'll see if he'll co-operate."

"Do we do that next?"

"No," Mason said. "We try to get some physical evidence next."

"Such as what?"

Mason said, "Madge Elwood took some dry clothes and shoes out to the lodge. Loring Lamont put them on. The trousers he had taken off, which were wet and muddy, were not left at the lodge. Therefore, someone must have put them in a car and taken them away—probably it was Madge Elwood. Yet they weren't in the car when she parked it."

"Therefore?" Della Street asked.

"Therefore," Mason said, "she took the things out and did something with them. Probably she transferred them to her own car. Now, what would she have done with them?"

"They may still be in her car."

"They may be in her car," Mason said, "and they may be in her garage. She probably drove her car into the garage. She may have taken out the trousers and the shoes. There's just one chance in ten that she did. Perhaps the chances are better than that. It may be an even-money chance."

"Do you suppose we can get in?"

"We may be able to," Mason said. "If her car is out of the garage, the garage may well be unlocked."

"And what about J. P. Lamont?"

"J. P. has a pretty good idea what happened," Mason said. "He doesn't want Arlene to tell her story, and he doesn't want to have that story corroborated by Madge Elwood. Therefore, he'd given Madge Elwood some sort of a bonus to get out of circulation and keep out of circulation until the case is finished."

"But what about Otto Keswick and Sadie Richmond?"

"Now there," Mason said, "we have an interesting situation. Bear in mind the phone call that Loring Lamont received there at the lodge just after the biscuits had been taken out of the oven and he and Arlene were ready to sit down to

150

eat. It was a call which caused him to change his entire plan of operations.

"That call was probably from Otto Keswick. Keswick and Sadie Richmond must have some sort of a partnership. It would be strange if, with Loring's nature, they didn't have some sort of a hold on him, something that would enable them to shake him down for a little blackmail when they needed the money.

"So Keswick telephoned and said, 'Look, Loring, Sadie and I need some money. We want five hundred bucks. We want it tonight. We're coming over to get it. I'll be there in half or three-quarters of an hour.' "

"Couldn't Lamont have told him to wait an hour or so?" Della Street asked.

"He may have tried to," Mason said. "We don't know what he said over the telephone, but we have a pretty good idea that Keswick and Sadie Richmond went out there. Loring Lamont knew they were coming, and so Lamont forgot all about the supper and the waltzing to the hi-fi and the seductive approach he had planned. He became crisply businesslike and efficient. He wanted what he wanted, and he wanted it before Keswick and Sadie Richmond got out there."

"And then they came out?"

"They came out after Arlene Ferris had gone home," Mason said. "They got a check from Loring Lamont, but by that time Loring Lamont was anxious to get rid of them because Madge Elwood was on her way out, and he wanted to get Otto Keswick and Sadie Richmond off the place before Madge arrived."

"Darned if it doesn't sound logical," Della Street said, excitement in her voice.

"So," Mason said, "we have three people who know that Loring Lamont was alive after Arlene Ferris left. We have Madge Elwood, we have Otto Keswick and we have Sadie Richmond."

"And none of them will want to involve themselves by testifying."

151

"None of them will want to become involved," Mason said.

"Look here, did Sadie and Otto get into a fight with him and . . . ?"

Mason shook his head. "Remember the fresh clothes. He didn't get those fresh clothes until after Madge Elwood arrived with his car."

Della Street thought it over, then became suddenly jubilant. "Chief," she said, "it all adds together! It fits into a perfect picture. You can blow the case into smithereens tomorrow morning and get Arlene Ferris acquitted."

"I can, if I can get the testimony," Mason said. "But remember this: Every one of those witnesses has lied or will lie. We can count on no co-operation from the authorities. We're going to have to dig up the evidence ourselves, and we don't have very much time to do it."

"And we start with Madge Elwood's garage?"

Mason nodded.

"Illegal?" she asked.

"That depends," Mason said. "If there's no lock on the door and we can simply open the door and walk in, we may be guilty of trespass, but we won't be guilty of burglary. We won't enter the place with felonious intent. We'll enter it for the purpose of discovering evidence."

"You don't think we could ring up Lieutenant Tragg and . . . ?"

Mason interrupted her by shaking his head. "Tragg would laugh at us."

"All right," she said, "let's go. I'm game."

"There's no reason for you to go in," Mason said. "You can sit in the car."

She said angrily, "What do you take me for? It you're going to take risks, I'm going to take them right along with you. In case you do find anything, you're going to need a witness, someone to corroborate your testimony. As a matter of fact, because you're the attorney for Arlene Ferris, you won't want to get on the stand yourself. You'd prefer to call me as a witness and then corroborate my testimony if circumstances made it necessary to do so."

152

"You win," Mason said. "Let's go."

They drove back to the apartment house. Mason turned at the entrance to the garages.

"The garages are numbered," Della Street said, "and there are cards to the right of each door."

They found Madge Elwood's garage.

Mason tried the door. It was unlocked.

"I think we'd better drive our car in here, Della," he said. "If we leave it outside and are prowling around it may attract attention. I'll drive in and then we'll close the door behind us and turn on the lights."

Mason drove the car into the garage. They closed the door. Mason found the light switch and turned it on.

Della Street said, "I'll take this side of the garage. You take the other side and we'll see what we can find—there's certainly a collection of junk here, a couple of old battered suitcases, a steamer trunk and a couple of tires."

Mason said, "The things we want may be in the trunk or the suitcases. How about that trunk, Della? Is it locked?"

Della Street tried the trunk and nodded. "It's locked," she said.

Mason said speculatively, "I don't know whether we dare to go and ask for a search warrant or not—you see, Della, so far we're working on surmise. We may have a pretty good idea what happened, but I'd like to get something positive to go on."

Mason paused to sniff the atmosphere in the garage. "It has that musty, mildewed smell beach places have that have been kept closed up," he said, "I wonder if . . ."

He broke off abruptly.

Della Street said, with alarm in her voice, "Chief!"

Mason put a finger to his lips for silence.

A car came to a stop just outside the garage door.

Mason and Della Street stood perfectly still. Abruptly the door was flung open. George Albert started to walk in, then recoiled with sheer surprise as he saw the car in the garage, saw Mason and Della Street standing there.

Lt. Tragg, who had been riding in Albert's car, opened the door and got out.

"Well, well," he said, "we seem to have stumbled on something of a jackpot, Albert."

George Albert said indignantly, "I told you they'd be trying to plant evidence. I want these people arrested, Lieutenant."

"On what grounds?" Mason asked.

"You know what grounds," Albert said. "You've been trying to plant evidence here. You've got some incriminating articles which were given you by Arlene Ferris, and you're trying to frame this thing on Madge Elwood. You've been trying to frame her right from the start. You got one of her skirts and tore it and left a piece out on the barbed wire. You left the skirt in Arlene Ferris' apartment. You've done everything you could to plant evidence that would drag Madge Elwood into this thing.

"You had your detective take pictures of her and go to Jerome Henley and try to bamboozle him into thinking that it was Madge he saw getting out of the car in front of the fireplug. You are now engaged in breaking into private property and planting evidence."

"We may be trespassing," Mason said, "but we aren't breaking in and we aren't planting anything. We're investigating."

"It's just as I told you, Lieutenant," George Albert said. "They're trying to drag Madge into this thing. I want this garage searched, and I want it searched now, for the purpose of finding whatever articles these people have planted here. Arlene Ferris went to Mason almost immediately after she killed Loring Lamont, and Mason has been planning to use Madge Elwood as a fall guy ever since. Now we've caught him redhanded."

Lt. Tragg regarded Perry Mason, slowly nodded. "We've caught him redhanded, Albert," he said. "I don't know just what the offense is that we've caught him at—we'll let the district attorney unscramble that one."

Mason said, "Tragg, can I talk with you for a moment in private?"

Tragg shook his head. "The only talking you're going to do is to the district attorney."

154

The officer turned to Albert. "Now look, Albert," he said, "I would advise you not to demand that we make an arrest. We've caught them here. That's enough. You and I will search the garage. We'll go through it from stem to stern. If we find any articles that they've planted we'll turn those articles over to the district attorney."

"Well," Albert said reluctantly, "I'm going to follow your advice—as soon as I knew they'd been around making inquiries I felt certain they'd try to plant something. I'm glad I got you on the job."

"I'm glad you got me on the job," Lt. Tragg said. "The district attorney is going to be glad you got me on the job. But let's use our heads a little bit."

"Whatever you say, Lieutenant."

Tragg said to Mason, "Albert will back his car out of the way. You and Miss Street can leave, Perry."

Mason said, "Tragg, I have reason to believe there are some articles of evidence in this garage. Don't let anyone give you any false notions. Go ahead and find them."

"And if you find them," Albert said, "you'll know who put them here."

"Never mind the argument," Tragg said to Albert. "Back your car up so they can get their car out. We'll start searching."

Albert got in his car, backed it out of the way.

Mason held his car door open for Della Street, walked around, got in beside her, backed the car out, turned it and drove out to the highway.

"Well?" Della Street asked.

Mason, his face grim, said, "There was a break that went against us."

"How bad a break?" she asked.

"Just about the worst break we could possibly get," Mason said. "If they find anything they'll swear that I planted it. You can rest assured that Hamilton Burger, the district attorney, will take personal charge of the case if they find anything."

"And it won't count against Madge Elwood?" she asked.

"Not now," Mason said. "It will count against Arlene Ferris."

"But look, Chief, you and I can both testify that . . ."

"You and I can both shout until we're black in the face," Mason said. "Our protestations will do no good. That's the trouble with being a citizen who has no authority and is trying to shortcut the law."

"But it wouldn't have done a particle of good if you'd gone to Lieutenant Tragg or the district attorney or the police or anyone else," Della Street said, almost crying. "You could have told them your suspicions and they'd have laughed at you. They wouldn't have done a thing."

"I know," Mason said, "but right now we're caught, and caught redhanded."

"Doing what?" she asked.

"That," he said, "is where we have a chance. We'll go to court tomorrow. If Hamilton Burger, the district attorney, walks in to take charge of the case personally we'll know that our deductions were correct, that they have found some evidence and that we're in just about the worst predicament we've ever been caught in."

Her hand moved out to rest on his. "All right, Chief," she said, "I'm in it with you. We're together in the thing."

Mason said grimly, "You're in it with me. We're both in the soup. But we aren't going to stay there. We're going to fight our way out."

Chapter 14

Precisely thirty seconds before ten o'clock, Hamilton Burger, the district attorney, came striding into the courtroom, and, with a perfunctory nod to Perry Mason, seated himself beside his deputy, Donald Carson.

A few seconds later, Judge Carleton Bayton took his place on the bench. Court was called to order, and the judge looked down at District Attorney Burger. "Was there something you wanted, Mr. Burger?" he asked.

Burger arose. "No, Your Honor. I am merely sitting in on the case of the People versus Arlene Ferris."

Despite himself, Judge Bayton couldn't control the expression of surprise. "I'm afraid I don't understand, Mr. District Attorney. This is a routine preliminary examination which is all but concluded. There remains only a few minutes of testimony this morning."

"Nevertheless," Burger said, "I am sitting in on the case. I may state to the court that I think there will be developments this morning which will change the entire complexion of the case. A matter has arisen since the adjournment of court which my office feels calls for the most thorough investigation, and in view of the fact that I may be called upon to take action in the matter, I wish to conduct that investigation personally."

Judge Bayton, plainly puzzled, said, "Very well. We will proceed with the case. Now, as I understand it, Mr. Prosecutor, the case had been continued to this morning with the idea that Peter Lyons, the officer whose testimony on direct examination had been stipulated by counsel, could be cross-examined by the defense"

"May I put it this way, Your Honor," Donald Carson said. "The People had not actually rested their case, but had announced their desire to do so. However, we are still putting on our case and we are not bound as to the witnesses we will call. However, the Court is quite right in stating that yesterday afternoon it was agreed that Peter Lyons, a police officer who had placed the first illegal parking ticket on Loring Lamont's automobile, would be present in court so that he could be cross-examined by the defense attorney.

"Mr. Peter Lyons is here, and I now ask him to take the stand—come forward and be sworn, Mr. Lyons."

Peter Lyons, a man in his early thirties, with high cheekbones, a crew haircut and lips set in a firm line of determination, came forward, held up his hand, was sworn and took his place on the witness stand.

Donald Carson said, "Mr. Lyons, you are a police officer on the metropolitan force. You were on duty during the evening of the fifth of this month, and you had occasion to put a tag for illegal parking on the automobile registered in the name of Loring Lamont, who is now deceased. Your testimony on direct examination was stipulated to, and this is the time fixed for cross-examination. Mr. Mason will now cross-examine you."

Mason arose and approached the witness. "Mr. Lyons, you put a tag on the Lamont automobile for illegal parking at about what time?"

"At about nine o'clock, according to my report."

"Where was the car parked?"

"Right in front of the fireplug near the apartment house at 9612 Endicott."

"What time did you go on duty?"

"At five o'clock."

"You were in a radio patrol car?"

"I was."

"Ordinarily do you pay attention to illegal parking?"

"At times, but . . . well, yes. In case of what we might call a flagrant violation, we issue a ticket. For instance, if a car is parked for a long time in front of a fireplug or perhaps if it is parked in front of a driveway we put on a ticket, then make it a point to swing back around within the next half

158

hour or so, and if the car is still there, we radio in to the dispatcher to have a tow car come and tow it away."

"Your district comprises the territory within which the Lamont car was parked?"

"Yes, of course."

"And you had been patrolling it since five o'clock in the afternoon?"

"Yes, sir."

"Did you get past this number on Endicott on an average of once an hour?"

"Now as to that, it's difficult to say. Sometimes we'd come down Endicott Way, sometimes one of the other streets. We were patrolling the district."

"But you did drive along Endicott Way several times between five o'clock, when you went on duty, and approximately nine o'clock, when you tagged the Lamont car?"

"Yes."

"During that time, on any of those trips, did you notice the Lamont car parked in front of the fire hydrant?"

"Of course," Lyons said, shifting his position on the witness stand, "we are primarily interested in parking violations, Mr. Mason. Therefore, I wouldn't be absolutely positive that . . ."

"That's not my question," Mason said. "I asked you if you noticed the Lamont car parked in front of the fireplug *prior* to the time you gave it the ticket."

"No, sir, I did not."

"The first time you noticed it parked in front of the fireplug you issued a ticket?"

"Yes, sir."

"Now, was there some reason why you were particularly interested in cars that were illegally parked in the territory?"

"There had been some complaint about illegal parking, and . . . well, yes, we had been instructed to keep an eye open for cars which were parked illegally. There was something of a drive on to stop illegal parking in that district."

"So that prior to nine o'clock on the evening of the fifth, during all of the times you had driven along Endicott Way, you had been on the alert for cars that were illegally parked?"

159

The witness hesitated for several seconds, then said, "Yes."

"Do you remember how many other automobiles you tagged that night for illegal parking?"

"I think there were two."

"Other than the Lamont car?"

"Yes."

"Now, you say there had been a problem in regard to illegal parking in the vicinity?"

"Yes."

"Do you know anything of the nature of that problem?"

"There are three apartment houses within three blocks. They are rather large apartment houses which do not have garages. There is a double vacant lot near one, which is used as a parking place for automobiles. As for the rest, cars are parked along the street, and after about six or seven o'clock in the evening the parking problem becomes very acute. As a result, many cars have been illegally parked and we have received complaints."

"You mean in front of fire hydrants?"

"Some of them were in front of fire hydrants. Most of the complaints, however, were for obstructing a driveway. Some complaints were from the owners of cars parked in the lot where another car was parked so that it was impossible to move the car because of the other car. There were numerous complaints and we were asked to try and clear up the situation."

"After nine o'clock you were on duty until how late?"

"Midnight."

"And you had occasion to drive through the district several times after nine?"

"Yes."

"Was the Lamont car still parked in front of the fireplug?"

"I don't know."

"Why don't you know?"

"Because I didn't actually see it, although I assume that it . . ."

"Never mind what you assume," Mason interrupted. "Let's talk about what you *know*."

160

"Yes, sir."

"Do you *know* that the Lamont car was parked in front of the fireplug between nine o'clock and midnight?"

"I don't know it, no, sir."

"Do you know that it wasn't?"

The witness hesitated.

"Yes or no," Mason said.

Lyons scratched his head, finally blurted, "I don't think it was."

"You're not certain?"

"Yes, I'm certain—that is, I'm as near certain as can be."

"What makes you certain?"

"I drove past there shortly before eleven o'clock, and I remember that just prior to making that swing around I made up my mind that if the cars I had tagged hadn't been moved I was going to phone in for a tow car and have them towed away before I went off duty."

"So you looked for the Lamont car then?"

"Now, Mr. Mason, I want to be absolutely fair. I remember that I had made up my mind that *if* I saw these cars illegally parked after I had ticketed them, I was going to call in for a tow car."

"And you didn't see the Lamont car illegally parked?"

"No."

"Did you look to see if it was still there?"

"Frankly, Mr. Mason, I have forgotten the exact sequence of events. I know that about the time we got to the address of Endicott Way a report came in of a prowler at the other end of my district, and we put on speed and went to take that call. Now, whether that call came in before we had passed the location of the Lamont car or afterwards I don't know. Of course, if that call had come in before, there is a possibility that I wouldn't have been as alert in regard to the illegal parking problem. I am now trying to recall certain things that happened. At the time, there was nothing particularly unusual about what was taking place. It is, therefore, simply a problem of trying to recall routine after a period of time. I'm sorry that I can't be more specific. I have tried to be fair. I have discussed this matter with the deputy district attorney

161

and with my superiors. I have consulted my notes. I have done the best I can, and I'm sorry that that is the most definite answer I can make. However, it is my considered opinion that, at about eleven o'clock, the Lamont car had been moved and was no longer in front of the fireplug."

"That's your best judgment?"

"That's my best judgment."

"Now then," Mason said, "what can you tell us about the other cars you tagged for illegal parking?"

Lyons made a gesture of throwing up his hands. "Nothing," he said. "All I know is, I issued tickets for illegal parking and turned the tickets in, in the usual course of routine. The cars were moved before I made my final checkup. Therefore, I can't tell you very much about them now. There has been no occasion for me to remember *them* or to refresh my recollection concerning them."

"Do you know where they were parked or what the nature of the violation was?"

"I remember that one of them was parked in front of a fireplug, but I think the other was parked so it was partially blocking a driveway. I can't be certain . . . no, wait a minute. There was one car that was double-parked. I remember now, the motor was running and the lights were on. Apparently the driver had just stepped out for a minute. I waited— oh, perhaps thirty seconds, and he didn't show up, so I tagged the car."

"And then what?"

"I drove down as far as the corner, then stopped my car and waited while I looked in my rearview mirror to see if the car that was double-parked was being driven away. It was, so I didn't pay any further attention to it."

"You went on around the corner and on about your business?"

"That's right."

Mason said, "If it hadn't been for the fact that this Lamont car was owned by a man who had been murdered on the date you tagged the car for illegal parking; if it hadn't been that your brother officers, who came on duty after you went off duty, assured you that the car was illegally parked all during the night in exactly the same place where you had tagged it; you wouldn't have had any question in your mind but what the car had been moved before you went off duty. Isn't that right?''

"I think that is right," Lyons said.

"And your best present judgment is that the car was moved between nine and eleven?''

"The witness again shifted his position. "I don't think I can tell you any more than what I have told you already, Mr. Mason.''

"Thank you," Mason said. "That's all.''

"I have no questions of redirect," Donald Carson said.

"Does that conclude the People's case?" Judge Bayton asked.

Hamilton Burger got to his feet. "Your Honor," he said, "it does not. A matter has come up which concerns me, not only as a prosecutor but as a member of the legal profession. Something has happened which I feel must be investigated in detail. I feel that an attempt has been made to fabricate evidence in this case, and I feel the facts should be so well established that proper steps may be taken. I wish to prepare a record at this preliminary hearing so that in case any of the witnesses should be spirited out of the country and not be available at the time of trial in the Superior Court, I can read the testimony of those witnesses into the record in accordance with the provisions of Section 686 of the Penal Code.''

"Isn't this rather an unusual procedure under the circumstances?" Judge Bayton asked.

"It is an unusual case, Your Honor, and is a case in which I wish to prepare a record which can be used either under the provisions of Section 686, or for the purpose of impeachment.''

"Very well," Judge Bayton said, "go ahead.''

"I wish to recall Lieutenant Tragg to the stand," Carson said.

Lt. Tragg, evidently carefully rehearsed as to the part he was to play, stepped briskly forward.

"You have already been sworn," Judge Bayton said to the witness. "Go ahead, Mr. Prosecutor.''

"Directing your attention to yesterday evening," Carson asked, "did you have occasion to go to an apartment house where one Madge Elwood has her residence? And apartment house known as the Kelsington Apartments in Santa Monica?"

"Yes, sir."

"Now, prior to that time had you taken any steps to identify the garment which has heretofore been marked for identification, the skirt with the cut in it?"

"I did. Yes, sir."

"What did you do?"

"I ascertained the store where the garment had been sold. I found that it was sold at a store in Santa Monica. I traced the code number of the cleaning establishment that was on the garment and found that number had been issued to one Madge Elwood, living at the Kelsington Apartments in Santa Monica. I may incidentally mention that when we arrested the defendant in this case she was living with Madge Elwood in this apartment; that is, she said she was visiting there, but she was actually living there with Madge Elwood at the time."

"So what did you do yesterday afternoon?" Carson asked.

"In the latter part of the afternoon, around five o'clock, I guess, I went to the Kelsington Apartments to investigate."

"Were you alone?"

"No, sir."

"Who was with you?"

"Mr. George Quincy Albert."

"Mr. Albert has previously been a witness in the case?"

"Yes, sir."

"And what did you do?"

"Mr. Albert had pointed out to me that . . ."

"Never mind any statements which were made outside of the presence of the defendant," Carson interrupted. "Those would be hearsay."

"I understand," Lt. Tragg said. "I didn't intend to state anything other than an incidental matter. However, I appreciate the point and will confine myself to what happened."

"And what did happen?"

164

"We went to the Kelsington Apartments. We first decided to look in the garage."

"You mean the garage that was rented to Madge Elwood along with the apartment?"

"That's right. The apartment house has a driveway which leads into a rather large area in the back. This area is in the form of a square, and three sides of that square are occupied by garages. Each garage is numbered for the apartment that goes with it, and names are put on the garages."

"And you went to the garage which had the name of Madge Elwood?"

"Yes, sir."

"What did you do?"

"Mr. Albert was driving the car. We came to a stop in front of the garage. Mr. Albert got out to try the garage door to see if it was locked."

"Was it locked?"

"No, sir."

"And Mr. Albert opened the garage door?"

"He did."

"What did you find inside of the garage?"

"We found an automobile in the garage, an automobile which was registered in the name of Mr. Perry Mason, the attorney for the defendant. We found Mr. Perry Mason and his secretary, Della Street, in the garage. They were out of the car at the time."

"Did you ask them what they were doing in there?"

"Mr. Albert accused them of planting evidence."

"And what did Mr. Mason say, if anything?"

"Objected to, if the Court pleases," Mason said. "This is hearsay. This conversation took place outside of the presence of the defendant. It is incompetent, irrelevant and immaterial."

"Mr. Mason, if the Court please," Carson said, "is the accredited representative of the defendant. The accusation was made in his presence, and his statement was in reply to that accusation."

Judge Bayton frowned, then shook his head. "It may be that counsel for the defendant has been indiscreet. It may be that he has been unwise, but the Court sees no reason why a conversation held in the presence of the attorney for the defendant, but without the defendant being aware of that conversation, should be binding upon her. The objection is sustained.''

"Very well. What did you do?" Carson asked.

"Well," Tragg said, "we first got rid of Mr. Mason and Della Street, and then we went to work in the garage."

"Doing what?"

"Searching it."

"For what?"

"For any evidence which might have been left there—*by anyone*.''

"What did you find?"

"We found a pair of mud-stained shoes. We found a pair of trousers with a rip down one seam of the trousers."

"Do you know who owned these articles?"

"I do now. I didn't then.''

"You made an investigation?"

"I did.''

'Take the shoes, for instance, Lieutenant. What did you do with reference to them?''

"I wired the factory, asking for the names of firms handling those shoes in the Los Angeles area. I may state that they were a very exclusive and expensive shoe. There were five shops which handled that shoe in Los Angeles. I finally located the name of the purchaser.''

"Who was that purchaser?"

"Just a minute," Mason said. "Quite obviously that's hearsay evidence. He is relying upon what some shopowner told him.''

Judge Bayton said, "Quite evidently it calls for hearsay evidence. However, can't we make certain stipulations here?''

"I am willing to stipulate as to statements which were made to Lieutenant Tragg by various persons, upon being assured that those statements *were* made," Mason said, "and subject to my right to bring the witnesses into court and cross-examine them if I so desire. I am willing to stipulate

166

that certain witnesses would have so testified on direct examination."

"Very well," Carson said. "Will you stipulate that the owner of one of the stores stated that he had Loring Lamont as one of his regular customers, that Loring Lamont customarily bought shoes of this style and make, and that these shoes were in his size? That is, they were the size purchased and worn by Loring Lamont?"

"That is a fact?" Mason asked.

"That is a fact."

"I will so stipulate."

"Will you stipulate that Mr. Loring Lamont's tailor identified these trousers as being part of the suit he had made for Mr. Loring Lamont, of identical material, and that the label in the waistband furnished a means of identification and that this tailor identified these trousers as being trousers which he had made for Mr. Loring Lamont in his lifetime?"

"That is a fact, is it?" Mason asked.

"That is a fact."

"I will so stipulate that the tailor would so testify, with the understanding that at any time I have the right of cross-examination if I so desire. I am simply stipulating as to what the testimony of these gentlemen would have been on direct examination."

"Very well," Carson said, and turned to Lt. Tragg. "Where were these articles found, Lieutenant Tragg?"

"In a locked trunk in the garage where we found Perry Mason and his secretary."

"You may cross-examine," Carson said to Mason.

"You stated," Mason said, "that you were looking for evidence which might have been planted by anyone, and, as I noticed the way you testified, you made a rather significant pause before saying the words *by anyone* and then you emphasized those words."

"That may be correct," Lt. Tragg said.

"When you said by anyone, I take it you meant what you said?"

"Exactly."

"The evidence could have been planted by me?"

"It certainly could have."

"And the evidence could have been planted by the defendant in this case?"

"It could have, although she was in jail at the time and . . . well, she could have, yes."

"And the evidence could have been planted by Madge Elwood?"

Lt. Tragg hesitated and then said, "I suppose it could have been."

"Thank you," Mason said. "That's all. No further questions."

"Now then, if the Court please," Carson said, "we are trying desperately to get in touch with Madge Elwood. It seems to be difficult to find her. However, with reference to the skirt which was identified by Lieutenant Tragg as being the property of Madge Elwood, I wish to call Bertha Anderson to the stand."

Bertha Anderson came forward and was sworn. Mason recognized her as the manager of the apartment house at Santa Monica.

"What is your occupation?" Carson asked.

"I am the manager of the Kelsington Apartments at Santa Monica."

"Do you know Madge Elwood?"

"I do."

"Does she live there?"

"She does."

"Do you know Mr. Perry Mason?"

"Yes. I have met him."

"When did you meet him?"

"I met him yesterday afternoon."

"And did you have a conversation with Mr. Mason?"

"I did."

"About Madge Elwood's apartment?"

"Yes."

"And did Mr. Mason ask if he could get in that apartment? If you would let him in with a passkey?"

"Objected to, if the Court please," Mason said, "on the ground that the question is incompetent, irrelevant and immaterial, that it is leading and suggestive, and further on the ground that counsel, well knowing the ruling of the Court in regard to conversations had with me outside the presence of the defendant, has deliberately tried by this leading question to prejudice the Court against the defendant's case.''

"The objection is sustained," Judge Bayton said, "and counsel is admonished. In fact, I wish to state, Mr. Prosecutor, that I consider the nature of this question was such as to constitute an attempt on your part to void and nullify the ruling of the Court. The Court has ruled, at least temporarily, that anything Mr. Mason may have said or done outside of the presence of the defendant is not binding upon the defendant.''

"He's her legal representative. He was acting on her behalf," Carson said angrily.

"The Court understands that, Mr. Carson, but the Court has ruled. You are familiar with the Court's ruling.''

Hamilton Burger arose ponderously. "If the Court please, may I be heard?''

"You may be heard, Mr. Burger.''

"We wish to state," Burger said, "that this is rather a serious matter, that it has come up out of a clear sky, so to speak. We have not had time to look up the authorities but I wish to state to the Court that I feel positive that we can find authorities indicating that as long as the defendant is represented by Mr. Perry Mason and as long as he is her duly constituted agent and attorney that the things he has done on her behalf are binding upon her. Furthermore, I feel that we should have an opportunity to show what these things are so that under the doctrine of agency we will force the defendant either to ratify the acts of her agent or to take steps to disaffirm those acts.''

"The Court has ruled. The Court's position is that the acts of Perry Mason and conversations which he has had outside the presence of the defendant are not binding upon her. Now, the Court can be in error in this matter and if you have any authorities which you wish to present, the Court will be glad to consider those authorities. In the meantime, however, the Court is going to adopt the position that you can only show

169

acts of the defendant and can only show conversations which occurred within the presence of the defendant. Otherwise they would be hearsay.''

"But, if the Court please," Hamilton Burger said, "here is a plain case, if I may speak frankly, where evidence which is exceedingly vital to the issues in this case has been planted by someone in the garage at the Kelsington Apartments. Mr. Mason, as the attorney for the defendant, was caught red-handed in that garage. It is at least a reasonable assumption that the only person who could have given those garments to him was the defendant in this case.''

"That's looking at it from the prosecution's viewpoint," Judge Bayton snapped. "On the other hand, you haven't as yet negatived the possibility that those garments were placed there by the most logical person of all, the person who rented that garage, Madge Elwood.''

"But where could she possibly have secured those garments?" Hamilton Burger asked. "She wasn't out at the lodge the night of the murder. She . . .''

"How does counsel know she wasn't?" Mason interrupted.

Hamilton Burger flushed angrily. "I don't choose to be interrupted," he said.

"And the Court would very much prefer not to have you interrupted," Judge Bayton said, "but since the interruption has been made, I will state that the question propounded by counsel for the defense is one which the Court intended to ask. How do you know she wasn't out there?''

"We'll prove it," Hamilton Burger said.

"Go ahead and prove it, then," Judge Bayton said, "and after your evidence has been concluded, if you then have sufficient circumstantial evidence to indicate that the articles in question *must* have been placed at the spot where they were found by any person acting under the direction and control of the defendant, you will have an opportunity to renew your offers of testimony. The Court will then permit you to recall these witnesses and ask these questions, provided you have in the meantime found some authorities to support your position.

170

"At the present time you are working only on an inference. The circumstances are not, in the opinion of the Court, strong enough to indicate a chain of circumstantial evidence necessarily connecting this defendant with the articles in question. However, the Court is very much interested in this phase of the inquiry and intends to cooperate in any way it can."

"Thank you," Hamilton Burger said, and sat down.

Carson turned to the manager of the apartment house.

"Were you the manager of the Kelsington Apartments on the fifth and sixth of this month?"

"I was."

"Were you acquainted with Madge Elwood on that date?"

"I was."

"Now, I am going to ask you if you saw Madge Elwood on the sixth of the month."

"I did."

"At what time?"

"I saw her several times."

"Did you see her in the evening? Early in the evening?"

"Yes."

"Did you have a conversation with her at that time?"

"Yes."

"Did you see the defendant on the sixth?"

"I did. Yes."

"And what happened at that time?"

"On the afternoon of the sixth Madge brought the defendant, Arlene Ferris, in with her. She was on her way to the elevator. She introduced me to Arlene Ferris and said Arlene was going to be visiting with her for perhaps a few days."

"Now, that was on the afternoon of the sixth?"

"Yes."

"And this conversation took place in the presence of the defendant?"

"Yes."

"Now, I show you a skirt, which has heretofore been marked for identification as People's Exhibit B-8, and I will ask you if you recognize that skirt."

"I do."

"Where did you see it?"

"I saw it on Madge Elwood on the sixth of the month."

"She was wearing that skirt?"

"She was wearing that skirt," Bertha Anderson said with positive finality.

"Now then, did you see her later on after that, on the sixth?"

"I did."

"At about what time?"

"It was early in the evening."

"What was Madge Elwood wearing at that time?"

"She was wearing that skirt."

"When you say that skirt, you are referring to the People's Exhibit B-8, the skirt which I am now holding in my hand?"

"Yes, sir."

"And where was she when you saw her?"

"She was in the lobby, going out of the apartment."

"Now, did you see her when she returned?"

"Yes."

"And what time was that?"

"That was quite a bit later—two or three hours later."

"And what was Madge Elwood wearing at that time?"

"She was wearing a different skirt. I remember noticing that she had gone out in one skirt and had returned in another. I started to say something and then held my tongue. After all, it was none of my business."

"Now, that was on the sixth of the month?"

"Yes."

"You may cross-examine," Carson said.

Mason turned to the witness. "Do you see people when they go and when they come out?"

"Quite frequently. I have an apartment which is back of the office, but I try to stay in the office so that I can see the lobby, particularly during the hours when the street door is kept unlocked."

"There's a desk there?"

"A sort of counter, yes."

"Any switchboard?"

"No. Tenants have their own phones or else use the phone booth in the corridor."

"Did you see Madge Elwood on the fifth of the month?"

"Yes, I saw her."

"In the evening?"

"I saw her when she came back from work in the early evening or late afternoon, and then I saw her again."

"When did you see her last on the fifth?"

"Objected to as incompetent, irrelevant and immaterial—not proper cross-examination," Carson said. "We have asked no questions about the fifth."

"I certainly have a right to test the recollection of the witness," Mason said.

"The objection is overruled. Proceed," Judge Bayton ruled.

"I saw her on the evening of the fifth about . . . oh, I guess it was about nine o'clock."

"And what, if anything, was she doing when you saw her?"

"She was going out."

"Did you see her come back that evening?"

"No."

"She came back after you had locked up for the evening?"

"Yes."

"And what time did you leave the lobby and lock up?"

"It was . . . I would say it was about eleven o'clock."

"Now, was Madge wearing this skirt which you have referred to, on the fifth?"

"No, she wasn't."

"How do you happen to remember this skirt so clearly?"

"Because I have one almost exactly like it. It is almost exactly the same pattern. Madge and I have commented on that from time to time."

"Madge left the apartment yesterday?"

"Yes."

"Carrying two suitcases?"

"Yes."

"Did you see her?"

"Yes."

"Did she tell you where she was going?"

"No."

"Did she tell you how long she expected to be away?"

"No."

"Wasn't that rather unusual?"

"Well, I don't inquire about a tenant's business as long as the rent is paid and . . . ."

"That isn't the question," Mason said. "Wasn't that rather unusual?"

"Well, yes, it was."

"Now then, since she left have you entered her apartment with a passkey?"

"Objected to as incompetent, irrelevant, and immaterial and not proper cross-examination," Carson said.

"I think it goes to show the bias of the witness," Mason said.

Judge Bayton hesitated. "I will permit the question."

"Did you enter the apartment?"

"Yes."

"With a passkey?"

"Yes."

"Were you alone?" Mason asked.

"Lieutenant Tragg was with me," she said.

"And what did you find in the apartment?" Mason asked.

"Now, if the Court please," Carson said, "that is definitely objected to as incompetent, irrelevant and immaterial and not proper cross-examination. We have not asked this witness anything about that at all on direct examination. This is going into an entirely different matter which will take the inquiry far afield."

"The Court is inclined to sustain that objection," Judge Bayton said. "I think perhaps the latitude on cross-examination has been ample to test the credibility of the witness."

"That's all," Mason said. "No further questions."

"If the Court please," Carson said, "I wish to introduce these trousers and the shoes as People's Exhibits, and at this time we renew our motion to show conversations with Mr. Perry Mason at the place where the articles were found. We feel that there has been sufficient circumstantial evidence to show that these articles were planted by Mr. Mason acting on behalf of the defendant.''

Judge Bayton slowly shook his head. "You haven't connected it up yet," he said.

"But if the Court please," Carson said, "these articles were the property of the decedent. It is quite evident that the defendant planned a story which would be well calculated to arouse the most sympathy on the part of a jury. She wanted to show that she had been attacked, that she had tried to defend her virtue, that she had been pursued through wet brush along a muddy road, that she had plunged through a barbed-wire fence.

"We have now shown, at least by inference, that Mr. Mason had Madge Elwood furnish a skirt which was deliberately left in the defendant's apartment after having been taken to the scene of the crime and a part of the skirt left on the barbed-wire fence. We have shown that this evidence could only have been planted on the evening of the sixth, some time after the murder had been committed, probably nearly twenty-four hours after the murder. That was for the purpose of substantiating the defendant's story.

"Now, we are also in a position to show that counsel secured possession of some of Loring Lamont's shoes and a pair of his trousers, that the shoes were deliberately muddied up and the trousers were dragged through wet brush and then ripped as though on a piece of barbed wire, and that counsel was actually caught redhanded in the act of planting those articles. We feel that under the circumstances there is every reason to believe that this was done as the result of a conspiracy between the defendant and her counsel and that the defendant is bound by his acts, that this attempt to fabricate evidence is an indication of guilt.''

"That's all very well," Judge Bayton said, "but how do you connect it up with the defendant? In the first place, how do you connect it up with Mr. Mason?''

"Mr. Mason and his secretary were caught redhanded," Carson said grimly.

"No, they weren't," Judge Bayton contradicted. "Their

hands weren't red at all. For all you know they hadn't been in that garage more than a matter of seconds. For all you know they were in there looking for evidence. Lieutenant Tragg has stated that he and George Albert went to the garage looking for evidence. Now suppose the sequence had been reversed? Suppose Perry Mason and Della Street had driven up a few seconds *after* Lieutenant Tragg and George Albert had entered the garage? Would you say that that was evidence that Lieutenant Tragg and George Albert were caught redhanded planting these articles in the garage?''

Carson's face flushed. "Certainly not."

"Well, it's exactly the same type of evidence that you have against Perry Mason," Judge Bayton said.

"But Perry Mason had reason to plant these articles. It was to his advantage—to the advantage of his client to have them discovered there."

"For all you know," Judge Bayton said, "it was to the advantage of George Albert to have the articles discovered there. It was to the advantage of the police to have the articles discovered there. I don't say that it was, I'm simply stating that for all you know it was. For all the Court knows, it was."

"Well, we're practical men," Carson said. "We know what happened."

"You know what you think happened," Judge Bayton said, "but what you think happened isn't binding upon the Court."

"Of course," Carson said with a trace of irritation in his voice, "if the Court expects us to produce eyewitnesses who will swear that they actually *saw* Perry Mason and Della Street open the trunk and put the garments in, we can't do it. Persons who commit a crime, particularly persons of intelligence, usually select a time when there are no witnesses."

Judge Bayton's face colored slightly. "The Court can well appreciate all that. The Court readily understands that usually crimes have to be established by inference, by circumstantial evidence. But the fact remains that the accused is entitled to certain presumptions. That's the function of a Court, to keep a sane perspective on the evidence.

"The Court feels that the evidence as it is now before the

Court is capable of several interpretations, one of the most logical being that the person who rented that garage is the one who put the garments in the trunk. The Court is not unmindful of the fact that the witness, Jerome Henley first identified Madge Elwood as being the person who was seen parking that automobile. Now I'm going to state frankly that the Court wants to get at the bottom of this. The Court would like to have Mr. Henley recalled to be questioned, not by counsel, but by the Court."

"Mr. Henley has returned to his place of business," Carson said. "Trying to get him back here would cause a delay. We understand and appreciate the desire of the Court to get this case disposed of."

"The Court has a very great desire to get this case disposed of," Judge Bayton said, "but the Court has an even greater desire to see that justice is done. I don't think it will take long to get Mr. Henley here and we can continue the case until he arrives."

"Perhaps," Mason said, "it will help clear this matter up if, while the Court is waiting for Mr. Henley to arrive, I can recall Lieutenant Tragg to the stand for further cross-examination."

"Very well," Judge Bayton said.

"Of course," Hamilton Burger said irritably, "this is only a preliminary examination. We only have to show that a crime was committed and that there are reasonable grounds to believe the defendant committed the crime."

"That's all you need to show at a preliminary examination," Judge Bayton said, "but this case has gone beyond that point. The good faith and the ethics of Mr. Perry Mason and his secretary have been questioned. The Court has no doubt but what the public press will make considerable capital out of this situation. Having gone this far, we're going to go the rest of the way.

"Lieutenant Tragg, will you return to the stand, please. I suggest to the bailiff that Mr. Henley be reached on the telephone and instructed to attend this Court."

Tragg came forward and took his place on the witness stand.

"Dirty dishes were found in the lodge by the police?" Mason asked.

"They were."

"They were taken to the police laboratory?"

"Yes, sir."

"They were processed for fingerprints?"

"Yes, sir."

"Did you find any fingerprints of the defendant on those dishes?"

"We did."

"Why did you fail to mention that fact in your direct testimony?"

"I wasn't asked."

"*Where* did you find the fingerprints?"

"On several of the dishes—particularly on the bowl which had been used for mixing the biscuit dough."

"On the coffee cups?"

"Well, no."

"On the plates?"

"We found one fingerprint on one of the plates."

"And, of course, you found fingerprints of the decedent?"

"Yes."

"Now then," Mason said, "isn't it a fact that you found fingerprints of at least one other person?"

Tragg hesitated a moment, then slowly nodded. "Yes, there were the fingerprints of at least one other person."

"Have you identified those prints?"

"Not as yet."

"And did you fail to mention the fingerprints of the defendant because the prosecutor had instructed you not to say anything about them for fear that my cross-examination would bring out the fact that another person's fingerprints were there?"

"I was told not to volunteer any information."

"Do you have the fingerprints of Madge Elwood?"

"No."

"Then you don't know that those other fingerprints were not those of Madge Elwood, do you?"

178

"We don't know whose they were. We do know they were not the prints of Sadie Richmond. We had thought that when she was putting the dishes away after they had been washed from the last time they were used, she might perhaps have left fingerprints. We therefore took her prints and compared them. They aren't her prints."

"Now then," Mason said, "when the defendant was telling you her story, did she tell you that the decedent had admitted to her that he had made a dummy telephone call? In other words, that he had gone into the lodge while she was still in the car, that he had called someone and asked that someone to call him back within a given number of minutes?"

"She told me that."

"Did you make an attempt to trace that call?"

"We made a check of all calls placed from the lodge on the night in question."

"And there again," Mason said, "you refrained from mentioning certain facts on your direct examination."

"There again," Lt. Tragg said, "I wasn't asked."

"You're being asked now," Mason said. "To whom did Loring Lamont place that call?"

"We don't know," Tragg said. "It was a station-to-station call. He simply called the number of the executive offices of the Lamont Company."

"The call wasn't placed to any particular person?" Mason asked, puzzled.

"Just to the office."

"All right," Mason said desperately, "what *other* calls were placed? After Loring Lamont found that he needed dry clothes and a new pair of shoes, whom did he call?"

"Now, just a moment before you answer that question," Carson said. "If the Court please, we object to that question as being argumentative, as assuming facts not in evidence, and not being proper cross-examination."

"The objection is sustained as to the last part of the question," Judge Bayton said. "The first part of the question will stand. Whom else did Loring Lamont call from the lodge?"

"No one," Tragg said.

179

"What!" Mason exclaimed in surprise.

"There were no calls," Tragg said. "No long-distance calls. Of course, we can't tell about incoming calls, but on the calls which were placed from that telephone there was only one call and that was a station-to-station call to the office of the Lamont Rolling, Casting and Engineering Company—the executive offices."

"And the time of that call?" Mason asked.

"The time was six-twenty-two, approximately the time when the defendant and the decedent arrived at the lodge, according to the story the defendant told us."

Mason half-closed his eyes in thoughtful concentration.

"Any further questions?" Judge Bayton asked.

"No further questions," Mason said.

"No questions," Carson said.

"We will take a ten-minute recess," Judge Bayton said. "We will reconvene just as soon as Jerome Henley arrives in court."

Judge Bayton left the bench. Hamilton Burger arose and, pointedly ignoring Perry Mason, strode into an anteroom.

Mason turned to Paul Drake and Della Street. "All right," the lawyer said, "we've got ten minutes to solve this case. Now what the hell happened? Loring Lamont *must* have made some arrangements to get dry trousers and shoes out to that lodge. How in the world could he have done it unless he telephoned?

"In view of the evidence they have now produced, we know that Arlene's story must be true. We know that he pursued her through the wet brush, that he slid down through the barbed-wire fence and tore his trousers when he did it. We know that he ran through the mud in the road, that his shoes were all muddy. Yet by the time he was killed someone else had appeared at the lodge. We are pretty certain now that that someone must have been Madge Elwood. But how did Madge Elwood get the dry clothes to him unless he telephoned her? How did she get into his apartment?"

Drake shrugged his shoulders. "He couldn't have contacted her by mental telepathy."

"There's only one answer," Mason said after a moment. "Madge Elwood must have called *him*."

"But why would she call him?"

"Because," Mason said, "she was close to him. She knew what Arlene had done. She had the number of the lodge and she called Loring Lamont at the lodge. We're fighting minutes on this thing, Paul. Get on the telephone. Call the telephone company. Tell them it's a matter of the greatest importance. Find out if Madge Elwood didn't place a call to that lodge on the evening of the fifth."

Drake said, "I'll try. I don't hope for much luck."

"Explain the circumstances to the manager of the telephone company," Mason said. "It's really a matter of life or death. Let's get at the bottom of this thing. See if you can get all the calls Madge Elwood placed from her apartment at about . . . now, let's see. Let's assume that Arlene left the lodge at about seven o'clock, that she drove back to her apartment, that she cleaned up, that she took Loring Lamont's car and put it in front of the fireplug, that she went back to her apartment, that she called Madge Elwood. That probably would be somewhere between—well, let's see, let us say around eight-thirty. Also, Paul, try and trace that call to the Lamont Company that was made at six-twenty-two. Let's see what happened on that."

"I'll try," Drake promised. "You haven't given me much time."

"That's because I haven't got it to give," Mason said.

Mason started pacing the floor of the courtroom, head thrust slightly forward, forehead creased in concentration.

After several minutes Mason whirled. "Della!" he said.

"Yes, Chief?"

"Go hunt up Paul Drake. He's telephoning. We've overlooked the vital point in the case."

"What is it?"

"Get the license number of the car that Peter Lyons tagged for double parking. Then get Paul to start his men running down the registration of that car, or it probably will be on the traffic ticket itself since the officer would take the owner's name from the Certificate of Registration which the law requires to be either on the steering post or on some portion of the automobile that is clearly visible.''

Della Street nodded, arose and left the courtroom.

Another five minutes passed.

Jerome Henley entered the courtroom, his manner that of a man who has been hurrying and is considerably exasperated.

Word was conveyed to Judge Bayton, and the judge once more took the bench.

Della Street came hurrying into the courtroom, seated herself beside Mason, and, as Jerome Henley was being called to the stand, said in an excited whisper, ''Chief, he struck pay dirt. Madge Elwood placed a long-distance call to the lodge. Then after that she called two Los Angeles numbers. Paul Drake is running down those numbers now. He had to go to another phone to contact his office and they're getting all the information on that traffic ticket issued by Peter Lyons on the car that was double-parked.''

Mason settled back in his chair. Slowly a smile came over his face. He turned to Arlene Ferris and gave her a reassuring wink just as Jerome Henley seated himself on the witness stand and Judge Bayton said, ''Mr. Henley, the Court wants to ask you some questions.''

''Yes, Your Honor.''

''Now,'' Judge Bayton said, ''I don't want counsel for either to side to interrupt. The Court is going to ask this witness some questions. Mr. Henley, try and put aside all prejudice from your mind. I am going to ask you to try and do something that perhaps may be more than human nature can readily do. I'm going to ask you to think back to the time when Perry Mason came into your store accompanied by a young woman whose name we now know was Madge Elwood. At that time you identified Madge Elwood as the woman you had seen getting out of the car.''

''I had been tricked by a previous . . .''

''Just a minute,'' Judge Bayton interrupted. ''Forget all this about having been tricked. You were *subsequently* convinced that you had been tricked and you resented it. You thought Mr. Mason had tried to trap you and tried to make

182

a fool of you. Now, I am going to ask you to get that entire thought out of your mind. I want you to think back to the occasion when Mr. Mason entered your store with Madge Elwood. How positive were you *at that time* that Madge Elwood was the woman you had seen getting out of the car?''

"I wasn't positive, I was tricked . . ."

"You said you were positive at that time. Now what caused you to say that?"

"Trickery."

"Mr. Henley," Judge Bayton said, "the Court is not entirely convinced that you *were* tricked. An *attempt* may have been made to trick you, but the Court is beginning to believe that it is quite possible that Madge Elwood actually was the person you saw getting out of that automobile."

Both Hamilton Burger and Carson jumped to their feet in protest. Judge Bayton motioned them to silence. "Now just a minute," he said. "The Court is doing this. I asked not to be interrupted by counsel for either side. I want you gentlemen to sit down and be quiet."

Judge Bayton turned to the witness. "The Court is here for the purpose of doing justice, Mr. Henley. The Court wants you to think back, to purge your mind of all prejudice against anyone."

Judge Bayton waited. There was a tense silence in the courtroom.

"Well," Jerome Henley said at length, "of course, Your Honor, I was convinced at the time that she was the person I saw getting out of the car. However, I had previously been shown her photograph and asked to identify that photograph. I had identified it, and that's where the trouble came in."

"But why did you identify the photograph?" Judge Bayton asked.

Jerome Henley stroked the angle of his chin thoughtfully. "Well, now, as to that," he said, "of course . . . well, the photograph looked something like that . . . looked exactly like the face of the person I had seen getting out of the car. That's because Madge Elwood and the defendant look a great deal alike and the photograph had been very cunningly taken . . ."

"It was a photograph of Madge Elwood?"

"Yes, there's no question about that."

"And it looked like the person you saw getting out of the car?"

"Very much."

"And then when you saw Madge Elwood you felt certain she was the person whose photograph you had seen?"

"That's the reason I made the identification."

"But are you prepared now to state on your oath to this Court that it was *not* Madge Elwood whom you saw getting out of the car? Now, think carefully, Mr. Henley. This isn't an attempt to trap you. This is simply an attempt on the part of the Court to get at the truth of the matter."

Henley closed his eyes, trying to concentrate. He continued to stroke the angle of his jaw with the tips of his fingers. "Well," he said at length, "they told me not to let Perry Mason make a fool of me, and I didn't intend to have him do so. But, of course, Your Honor, when you come right down to it, when I saw that picture of Madge Elwood . . . well, at the time I *thought* that was the young woman I saw getting out of the car. Then when I saw Madge Elwood, of course there had been a certain amount of suggestion and . . . well, when I saw her I thought she was the woman, all right."

"You don't think so now?"

"Well, now," Henley said, "the situation is different. I look at the defendant and I think she's the woman, but of course I've been shown *her* picture, too."

"Forget all the picture business," Judge Bayton said. "Try and think back. Try and visualize the young woman who got out of the car. Was it Madge Elwood or was it the defendant in this case?"

Jerome Henley looked up at the judge and finally blurted out, "When you put it that way, Your Honor, I don't know. When I first saw Madge Elwood I was pretty certain that was the young woman. Then I became certain it was the defendant, but when you put the thing that way—when you put it up to me in just that way, I just don't know."

"That's all," Judge Bayton said. "Now, if counsel for

either side wants to question the witness, they can. But as far as the Court is concerned this witness made a positive identification of Madge Elwood. He made it under circumstances that impress the Court. He now says he doesn't know. Does counsel for either side want to question him?"

"No questions," Mason said.

Hamilton Burger and Carson engaged in a whispered conference, then Hamilton Burger said, "No, Your Honor, no questions."

Mason said, "I have one more question of Lieutenant Tragg. You don't need to resume the stand, Lieutenant. You can answer it from right where you are in the courtroom. Among other things that you didn't mention in your testimony, was there anything about the blood alcohol of the body of Loring Lamont?"

Tragg said, "I didn't run that test myself. That was done by the autopsy surgeon, Dr. Draper."

"But you know what the results were," Mason said. "What were they?"

"Well," Tragg said, "I understand the blood alcohol percentage was point one nine."

"That," Mason said, "would indicate a considerable degree of intoxication, would it not?"

Tragg said dryly, "It would."

"Considerably more than a man of his size could get from ingesting one cocktail or two or three?"

"Probably four, five or six," Lt. Tragg said.

"I'll ask the prosecution to stipulate that Dr. Draper would so testify if he had been asked," Mason said.

Again Carson and Hamilton Burger had a whispered conference.

"Don't you know?" Judge Bayton asked.

"Yes, Your Honor," Carson said with poor grace. "We know. We will so stipulate."

"But obviously," Judge Bayton said, "this is changing the complexion of the case materially."

"I don't see why," Hamilton Burger said. "The Court is acting on what I think is an erroneous assumption."

"What's that?"

"That the defendant is telling the truth. We don't feel she is telling the truth. We feel she went out there deliberately and was there for a long time with the decedent, that they had drinks, that this defendant wasn't at all averse to any familiarities, that she led the decedent on, that she didn't object to his getting drink and she didn't object to his taking liberties."

"Then how did it happen the decedent had in his clothing a part of the distributor from the defendant's car?"

"Because she placed it there after his death. *She* was the one who deliberately disabled her car so Loring Lamont would offer her a ride. From that point, she led him on."

"Then why did she run away, dash down the road and plunge through the barbed-wire fence?"

"I don't know that she did, Your Honor."

"Well, the clothes belonging to the decedent indicate that she did."

"After all," Hamilton Burger interposed irritably, "the Court doesn't need to go into all this. The function of the Court is only to find out *at this time* if there is reasonable ground to believe the defendant was connected with the commission of a crime."

"That's all very true from a standpoint of abstract law," Judge Bayton snapped, "but here we have a young woman whose reputation is at stake, whose liberty is at stake. A lot of evidence has been introduced and you have now made it a point to question the integrity of Mr. Perry Mason, an officer of this court.

"If the defendant is guilty, if Mr. Mason was guilty of planting evidence, the Court wants to find it out. If they are innocent, the Court wants to establish that fact. The function of a court of law, Mr. District Attorney, is to see that justice is done. In the opinion of this Court, that is far more of an obligation on the Court than to comply with the letter of the law in regard to a preliminary examination."

Paul Drake hurried into the courtroom, pushed a piece of paper in front of Mason. "All right, Perry, here it is," he whispered. "Madge Elwood called the lodge. Then she called two numbers. One of them was the number of George

Quincy Albert and the other was the number of the apartment of Edith Bristol. I've traced the call from the lodge to the executive offices of the Lamont Company. Lamont simply called up the switchboard operator and told her to call him back in exactly seven minutes and as soon as he answered to hang up the phone without staying on the line to listen to what was being said.''

Judge Bayton said, ''Are there any further witnesses?''

''We have none, Your Honor,'' Hamilton Burger snapped. ''That's the prosecution's case. We rest, and regardless of what may happen in the Superior Court, we wish to point out that there is more than ample evidence to bind this defendant over for trial.''

''Does the defense have any evidence?'' Judge Bayton asked.

Mason got to his feet. ''We have some evidence, Your Honor. It will take us a little time to produce it unless the district attorney's office wishes to stipulate. However, it is a matter of record, and the records can be verified by the Court or by the prosecution.''

Paul Drake whispered to Della Street, left the courtroom.

''What is this evidence?'' Judge Bayton asked.

''Let us assume,'' Mason said, ''that the story of the defendant is true. Loring Lamont found himself marooned out at the lodge. He was wearing wet clothes. He had torn the trousers. He had been repulsed in his advances. He was angry, he was wet, he was frustrated, and he had been outwitted. His automobile had been—well, borrowed.

''We only need to put ourselves in his position to find out what he would do.''

''Just a moment, Your Honor,'' Hamilton Burger interrupted. ''We object to any argument at this time. If the defense has any evidence, let them put it on. After the evidence is in, counsel can use his eloquence all he wants—and then *we'll* have an opportunity to point out our interpretation of the facts.''

Judge Bayton nodded. ''I think as a matter of procedure the prosecutor is correct, Mr. Mason. I think argument as such should come at the close of your evidence. However, the Court will state that the Court will welcome such argument at that time.''

"I was merely trying to show the background, Your Honor,'' Mason said.

"I think the Court understands the background. What's your evidence?''

"Simply this,'' Mason said. "I had thought that Loring Lamont would call someone to bring him clothes and a car and I was very frankly surprised when the record of long-distance calls showed he hadn't done so. The reason for that is now . . .''

"Here we go again,'' Hamilton Burger shouted. "Counsel is continuing with this same type of argument after the Court has admonished him. We assign this as misconduct and an attempt to circumvent the ruling of the Court.''

"The Court agrees with the district attorney,'' Judge Bayton said sternly. "Mr. Mason, if you have any evidence, present it. Save your argument until after your evidence has been presented and please comply with the rulings of the Court.''

"Yes, Your Honor,'' Mason said. "The evidence is simply this. The records of the telephone company show that Madge Elwood called Loring Lamont at the lodge from her apartment on the evening of the fifth. It shows that immediately after she'd finished talking with the lodge she made two calls. One of them was to the number of George Albert and the other one was to the number of the apartment of Edith Bristol, the personal secretary of J. P. Lamont.''

Paul Drake again came hurrying into the courtroom.

"If I may have the indulgence of the Court for just a moment,'' Mason said. Drake handed Mason a paper, Mason looked at the paper, then smiled at the Court and said, "And the records also show that the car which was tagged by Peter Lyons for being double-parked was a car that was registered in the name of Edith Bristol. Those are matters of record and we ask the prosecution to so stipulate in order to save time.''

"Will the prosecution so stipulate?'' Judge Bayton asked.

"The prosecution will so stipulate only on the assurance

of counsel for the defendant that he knows such facts to be true.''

"I know such facts to be true," Mason said, "only because of telephone conversations had by Paul Drake, the detective, with the officials of the telephone company and a hasty investigation of the parking ticket issued by Officer Lyons. However, I am assured that such are the facts and if there is to be any question about them I would like to have a continuance until they can be verified.''

"We object to such a continuance," Hamilton Burger said, "and we don't feel that we should stipulate in view of the situation.''

"You will stipulate, will you not," Judge Bayton asked, "subject to the proviso that if any of the facts should turn out to be incorrect those facts can be called to the attention of the Court?''

"We'll make that stipulation," Hamilton Burger said with poor grace, "however, we can't see the relevancy of all this.''

"You object to the evidence on the ground that it's incompetent, irrelevant and immaterial?" Judge Bayton asked.

"We do," Hamilton Burger said.

"The objection is noted," Judge Bayton ruled. "Now, Mr. Mason, the Court would very much like to hear argument upon the objection of the prosecution. This will be an opportunity to present your theory of the case.''

Judge Bayton sat back, the ghost of a smile on his lips, his hands across his stomach, the fingers interlaced.

Hamilton Burger, realizing the trap into which he had walked, arose as though to make some objection, then slowly sat down.

"Mr. Mason will proceed," Judge Bayton said.

Mason said, "If the Court please, the situation is simply this. Looking at it from a logical standpoint, Loring Lamont must have returned to the lodge after his car had been taken by the defendant. He angrily dumped the ham and eggs down the garbage disposal; he probably didn't care for coffee at that time. He poured himself several drinks. He didn't know exactly what to do. He was debating how to proceed. He didn't know where his car was. He didn't know whether the

189

defendant had gone to lodge a criminal complain against him or not.

"The defendant in the meantime drove back to town, parked Loring Lamont's car in front of a fireplug and telephoned her friend, Madge Elwood, telling her what she had done. Madge Elwood knew Loring Lamont. There is no purpose at this time in exploring the intimacy of that relationship. Madge Elwood was a modern young woman with a certain amount of independence and a tolerant outlook on life. She probably telephoned Loring Lamont at the lodge and said, in effect, 'Arlene Ferris telephone me. You certainly went at her pretty rough. She took your automobile and left it parked in front of a fireplug. What do you want me to do?'

"And at that time Loring Lamont told her, 'What I want you to do is to bring the car out to me, contact someone who can go to my apartment and get me a clean pair of slacks, a dry pair of shoes, and you can bring them out here.'

"Thereupon," Mason said, "Madge Elwood made two calls. One of them was to a person whom she wanted to accompany her out to the lodge because in Loring Lamont's mood she didn't care to go out there alone. The other one was to the person who was to go to Loring Lamont's apartment and get him the articles of wearing apparel he had requested. Obviously that would be a person who had a key to the apartment, a person who was sufficiently intimate with Loring Lamont to be able to go to his apartment at will, and quite apparently that person was either George Albert or Edith Bristol.

"One of those persons accompanied Madge Elwood to the lodge. The other person went to the apartment and got the wearing apparel.

"We have to use inference to determine which was which.

"We know that parking space was at a premium around the apartment. We know that cars were parked at such times in front of driveways and in front of fireplugs. The person who went to the apartment of Loring Lamont to get the articles in question was in a hurry and didn't have time to park the car a long distance from the apartment and walk. That

190

person took a chance on double-parking. The car that was double-parked in front of the apartment was tagged by Officer Lyons, at the same time he tagged the Loring Lamont car. That car belonged to Edith Bristol.

"If, therefore, my surmise is correct, Edith Bristol was the one who took out the garments to Loring Lamont, and George Albert was the one Madge Elwood telephoned when she wanted someone to escort her out there."

Edith Bristol, arising, came stalking forward. "May I make a statement to the Court?" she asked.

"This is out of order," Hamilton Burger protested.

"The district attorney will please be seated," Judge Bayton said. "What sort of statement did you wish to make, young woman?"

"I am Edith Bristol, the private secretary to Jarvis P. Lamont," she said. "I am tired of deception. I am tired of intrigue. I probably would have confessed anyway, but there's no use trying to carry on the deception any more. I killed him."

"Come forward and take the witness stand," Judge Bayton said. "Now, young woman, I want you to understand that anything you say can be used against you. You are entitled to the benefit of counsel. You don't have to make any statement at this time. Do you wish the Court to appoint an attorney to represent you, or do you wish to call on . . ."

She shook her head. "I only want to get it over with, Your Honor."

"Very well," Judge Bayton said, "go on. Get it over with. Tell us what happened."

She said, "Loring Lamont was a fascinating and influential man. He swept me off my feet when I came to work for the Lamont Company and I suppose the fact that he was influential had something to do with it. I became intimate with him. I thought he was going to marry me. He assured me that he would as soon as he could condition his father's thinking. In the meantime he told me that he would manipulate things so I could get in his father's office as a private secretary and that would give me a chance to, as he expressed it, 'soften up the old man.' I soon found that Loring Lamont

191

was either having an affair or preparing to have an affair with another young woman in the office, Madge Elwood. Madge Elwood was a very broad-minded, modern young woman. I went to her and put the cards on the table. Madge Elwood told me that up to that point she and Loring Lamont were good friends, that that was all. She assured me the situation hadn't progressed beyond that point, and that she didn't intend to let it progress beyond that point. She told me that she actually was becoming interested in George Albert, the office manager. She told me that in order to simplify the problem as far as I was concerned, she would leave the employ of the Lamont Company. She did so.

"She pointed out to me, however, that an attractive young woman who dressed in the modern style in order to accentuate her sexual charms or at least disclose them enough to attract the masculine eye certainly shouldn't resent masculine attention. She was, as I state, very tolerant and very broad-minded.

"I happen to know that Loring Lamont continued to try and date her, that she became more and more interested in George Albert and that Loring's attempts to date her were fruitless, although she did like him. She wanted to be friends with him but there was nothing platonic about Loring Lamont's relationships with the opposite sex. More and more I was forced to close my eyes to his affairs with women.

"On the night of the fifth Madge Elwood telephoned me. She seemed rather amused. She said that Loring Lamont had taken Arlene Ferris out to the lodge and had become a little impetuous, that Arlene had grabbed his automobile and gone off in it, leaving Loring Lamont on foot. Loring was terribly afraid that his father would find out about the situation. It seems that his father had taken Loring to task on several occasions about his immoral conduct and particularly had ordered him not to use the lodge under any circumstances for any of his affairs.

"Madge told me that Loring Lamont had asked her to instruct me to go to his apartment and get trousers and shoes. I had a key to his apartment. I think I was the only person besides himself who did.

"I drove at once to his apartment. I double-parked and ran up and got the shoes and trousers. When I came down there was a tag for parking violation on my car. I hurried out at once to the lodge.

"Loring Lamont was there. He was offensively, obnoxiously drunk. I gave him the trousers and shoes. He changed into dry clothes. I fixed some coffee in an attempt to sober him up. I also cooked ham and eggs in order to induce him to eat. There was a pan of cold biscuits. I warmed them up. We had ham and eggs together.

"He became exceedingly obnoxious. He taunted me with the fact that I had been, as he called it, a pushover. He said I had a nice figure but no glamor. I remember he said that the newness had worn off his affair with me, and that he was tired of having to try to deceive me whenever he saw a new person who appealed to him. He then boldly and brazenly announced his determination to get in his car and go to the apartment of Arlene Ferris and force her to apologize for stealing his car. He said if she wasn't 'nice' to him he'd have her arrested for car stealing. He said that he liked women who were difficult, that he was really going to make her pay for what she had done.

"I was terribly upset and he was in a beastly mood. I finally slapped him. Then he started to choke me. I ran into the kitchen and tried to get out the kitchen door. It was bolted and locked. There was no way out. He was between me and the door back to the living room. I kept a table between us. By that time he was in a murderous rage. I grabbed a butcher knife. He lunged toward me, stubbed his toe and missed. As he went by me, half falling, I lashed out with the butcher knife. I didn't know I had killed him. I did know the knife had gone into his back. I had no idea it would go in so easily. I was frightened at what I had done, but I had no idea he was even seriously wounded. I only hoped the knife thrust would slow him down enough so I could escape further abuse. I ran into the living room.

"He tried to chase me but stumbled and fell by the table. I dashed out, got in my car and drove away."

There was silence in the courtroom.

193

Mason said quietly and with consideration in his voice, "Miss Bristol, did he tell you anything about a check for five hundred dollars?"

She nodded. "That was why he became so impetuous with Arlene Ferris. He said that he had intended to play it slow and easy for a while but that Otto Keswick, who with Sadie Richmond had been blackmailing him for some time over certain of his affairs he didn't dare have come to the attention of his father, had called him and said they needed five hundred dollars at once and would be out within half an hour."

Mason turned to the back of the courtroom. "Now perhaps we'll hear from you, Mr. Albert," he said.

Albert arose and said with dignity, "As it happens, Madge Elwood is my wife. We were married last night in Las Vegas. I flew back here in order to be present in court. As the husband of Madge Elwood I cannot be called upon to testify against her, nor can she be called upon to testify against me."

Albert sat down.

Judge Bayton looked at the district attorney, then at Carson, then at Mason. "Does the defense have any further evidence?"

"None, Your Honor."

"The case against the defendant is dismissed," Judge Bayton said. "The Court orders Edith Bristol into custody. The Court does so with reluctance. The Court feels that this young woman has told her story with great sincerity. It is a story which has made a deep impression upon the Court. The Court has every reason to believe that a jury will believe that story and that Loring Lamont was killed in self-defense. Court is now adjourned."

Chapter 15

Perry Mason, Della Street, Paul Drake and Arlene Ferris sat in Mason's office.

Arlene Ferris, almost hysterical with joy, was red-eyed from crying, and Della Street sat beside her holding her hand, patting it reassuringly from time to time.

"Well," Mason said, tossing his brief case on the desk, "there's another case out of the way."

"It's just a case to you," Arlene Ferris said, "but it's my whole life."

Mason looked at her sympathetically.

"It's his whole life, too," Della Street said. "His life's work is to see that justice is done, not only in one case, but in *all* his cases."

"Come on, Perry," Paul Drake said, "just what happened?"

"It's simple," Mason said. "Loring Lamont was a wolf. He deliberately planned a conquest of Arlene. He would do it nicely if he could. He would do it the hard way if he couldn't do it the easy way. Apparently he had had quite a bit of experience and he knew the California law, that a woman who becomes the complaining witness in a rape case can be questioned about past indiscretions.

"That gives an unscrupulous man with unlimited money to hire detectives a very considerable leeway.

"However, Otto Keswick put the bite on Loring, told him he would be out in half an hour. Loring decided to speed up operations. We know what happened.

"Sometime later, Madge Elwood had telephoned and told him she'd bring his car out. She also told him she'd arrange to get dry clothes for him, but Madge Elwood didn't have any intention of being placed in the same predicament Arlene

195

had. So she called for her fiancé, George Albert, to go with her. In the meantime, she called Edith Bristol. Edith went to the apartment, got the things Lamont wanted and went out to the lodge. Madge deliberately gave Edith a head start.''

''Why didn't Edith leave her car and drive Loring Lamont's car out to the lodge?'' Drake asked.

Mason said, ''Nothing was said about that. Lamont didn't want either to drive Edith home or to be saddled with her for the rest of the evening. Remember the evidence shows he had been drinking heavily. When Madge telephoned him he told her to have Edith, who lived close to his apartment and had the only other key, go and get some dry clothes and bring them out. Then Madge was to bring his car out and he planned to have Edith drive Madge back. Loring Lamont didn't intend to let Arlene get away with her coup. He probably planned to drive to her apartment and surprise her. This time he didn't intend to let her throw a chair.''

''And the clothes?'' Drake asked.

''By the time Madge and George Albert got out there,'' Mason said, ''Loring Lamont was dead. I'm satisfied that they found the body and simply decided to say nothing about it. They felt that the police would be without any clues, and they wanted to keep out of it. So they decided to take Lamont's discarded clothes and hide them. In that way they felt they could keep anything from coming out about what had really happened. Madge was saving Edith's good name, Arlene from publicity, and protecting herself at the same time. So Madge simply returned Lamont's car to the place where Arlene had parked it. She and George Albert felt no one would ever know what had happened after Arlene left.''

''Isn't that a crime,'' Drake asked, ''failing to report finding a murdered man? Can't they be booked on that?''

''Sure, it's a crime,'' Mason said grinning, ''provided the D.A. can prove it.''

''He can't prove it?''

Mason shook his head. ''They're married. Burger can prove Madge Elwood phoned Edith to go out to the lodge, but he can't prove Madge Elwood ever went out there. Thanks to the way the police tried to brainwash Jerome Henley, there's no way of proving Madge was the young woman who parked Loring Lamont's car. At first Henley said she was, then he said she wasn't, then he swore he didn't know. It's a case of the prosecution kicking its own case out of the window by trying to influence a witness."

"How about the check Loring Lamont wrote out there at the lodge?" Della asked. "If Otto and Sadie were so anxious to get it why didn't they cash it?"

"It's almost a sure bet," Mason explained, "that they wanted this check to finance some gambling activities of their own. I'd be willing to wager that when the facts are known we'll find that pair turned the check over to some bookmaker that night. The next day before the check was presented at the bank this person learned of the death of Loring Lamont and knew the check was worthless. A bank can't pay any check drawn on the account of a depositor once the bank knows the man is dead. So the holder of the worthless check tore it up rather than get mixed up in a situation where he'd have explanations to make."

"How about the other check, the one from Jarvis P. Lamont?" Della Street asked. "The one he gave Madge Elwood?"

Mason said, "He did that so she could get married and so neither she nor Albert could be called as a witness. Jarvis P. Lamont wanted to protect the so-called good name of his son if he could. Apparently he was willing to sacrifice Arlene in order to do it."

"But," Della Street asked, "how in the world did Jarvis P. Lamont know all that had happened?"

Mason grinned. "I think we have to concede, Della, that Madge Elwood is a very astute young woman as well as a good-looking one."

"Yes," Paul Drake chimed in, "that makes me wonder what you were talking about all that time she was changing her skirt in Arlene's apartment. It seems to me you were gone quite a spell on that trip. What *were* you talking about?"

Mason winked at Della Street. "Books, Paul," he said.

"Next time," Drake observed, "you'd better use me to do your leg work."

"It was brain work," Mason corrected.

About the Author

Erle Stanley Gardner is the king of American mystery fiction. A criminal lawyer, he filled his mystery masterpieces with intricate, fascinating, ever twisting plots. Challenging, clever, and full of surprises, these are whodunits in the best tradition. During his lifetime, Erle Stanely Gardner wrote 146 books, 85 of which feature Perry Mason.